A MIDSUMMER NIGHT'S SCREAM

ALSO BY HP MALLORY:

PARANOMAL WOMEN'S FICTION:
Haven Hollow
Midlife Mermaid
Midlife Spirits

PARANORMAL ROMANCE:
The Underworld Series
Arctic Wolves
Wolves of Valhalla
Lucy Westenra

EPIC FANTASY ROMANCE:
Lily Harper
Dulcie O'Neil
Here to There

PARANORMAL ADVENTURE:
Chasing Demons
Dungeon Raider

REVERSE HAREM:
My Five Kings
Happily Never After

DETECTIVE SCI-FI ROMANCE:
Alaskan Detective

A MIDSUMMER NIGHT'S SCREAM

Book 7 of the Dulcie O'Neil Series

H.P. Mallory

A MIDSUMMER NIGHT'S SCREAM

Book 7 of the Dulcie O'Neil Series

By

HP MALLORY

Copyright ©2018 by HP Mallory

Acknowledgements:

To my mother: Thank you for everything you do.

To my son: Thank you for making me the proudest mom out there! I adore you.

To Len: Thank you for being so understanding about me getting this book done! Your encouragement doesn't go unnoticed. I love you.

To my editor, Teri, at www.editingfairy.com: Thank you for always making my books stronger.

To my beta reader Evie from Paromantasy: Thank you for always being read, willing and able to read my books!

To Dina Marie: Thank you for all your help with the cop bits in this book! You're awesome!!

To Tara Lynn Ryan: Thank you so much for entering the contest to come up with the title for this book. It's fantastic!

ONE

Leaning back in my chair, I propped my ankles up on the desk in front of me. Then I pulled my arm back and threw the red rubber ball against the opposite wall as hard as I could. It hit the wall, bounced against the floor, and banged into the ceiling before hitting the floor again. Then, as if seeking refuge, it disappeared underneath the fake ficus tree that was doing nothing more than collecting dust in the corner of the room.

"Dulcie!" I heard Sam's shrill voice coming from the office adjacent to mine. "Stop it! You're driving me crazy!"

Sam was my best friend and also a very gifted witch—one who, apparently, didn't like the repetitive sound of a rubber ball banging against the wall. I huffed out a breath of indignation while admitting to myself that I, too, *had* already tired of my incessant game.

Looking for something else on which to focus, I turned my attention to the large window, which took up most of the wall beside me. The city of Splendor, California, was splashed with the brilliant colors of fall, and the leaves of the maple trees had just started to yellow and brown. A wind whipped through the branches, and the leaves shuddered, a few of them breaking free and drifting down to the ground below.

"I'm sure there are more productive things you *could* be doing," Sam said, her voice now coming from directly behind me.

I wheeled around in my chair and faced her with an eager frown. "Well, I *was* in the middle of one rather productive thing, but *someone* interrupted me." I arched an eyebrow just for the hell of it. "I won't mention any names though."

"Clearly, you're in need of something useful to occupy yourself," she said as she crossed her arms over her modest chest. She tapped her index finger against her lips like she did whenever she was busy pondering something. "Do I need to make another Starbucks run?" she asked, a smile brightening her pretty face.

Yep, Sam was definitely attractive with her plump lips, large, doe-like, brown eyes and chocolate-colored hair, which she always wore in a tidy bob. The comparison to a deer was actually a pretty good one. Looking at Sam's incredibly long, thin legs and her overall graceful appearance, she resembled Bambi in human form. Well, in human *girl* form, that is.

If Sam could be compared to Bambi, I would have been more along the lines of Thumper. I'm only five-foot-one, but although I'm small, I'm strong and toned since I insist upon keeping myself in shape. In my line of work, you have to be quick on your feet; it could mean the difference between life and death. And since I've only been alive for twenty-six years, that difference is a hefty one for me.

"I've already had four cups of coffee today, and it's only," I glanced at the clock on the wall opposite me before looking back at Sam again, "eleven." My hand twitched as I longed for my little red ball to throw again. "Any more caffeine and I'll probably have a heart attack."

Sam didn't say anything right away as she entered my office. She pulled out one of the guest chairs on the opposite side of my desk. Taking a seat, she studied me in that way of hers, which meant I probably wouldn't like whatever was about to emerge from her mouth. "I know this is hard for you, Dulcie," she started in her *mom* tone. "You've never been the type who can just sit around."

"Yep," I agreed with a sigh because there was really no denying my current state of boredom. After receiving express orders to man Headquarters, otherwise known as the ANC (Association for Netherworld Creatures), I had to remain rooted here for the time being. And Sam was right—desk jobs weren't for me.

"But you realize you're the only one who is qualified to run this office in Knight's absence?" Sam continued, nodding her head like she was also trying to convince me in sign language.

Knight Vander was the head honcho of the ANC division in Splendor. Technically, he was my boss, but personally, he was also my boyfriend. Now, however, he was absent and had been for the past two months. Not that I was particularly upset about it ...

I took a deep breath and sighed it out again. "I really don't need a pep talk, Sam," I grumbled. Truth be told, I wasn't good with emotional stuff; I never had been. Instead, I preferred the stark reality of cold, hard facts. Cold, hard facts couldn't cry and give me a guilt trip. "All I really need is to get the hell out from behind this desk so I can start patrolling the streets again."

"You've never been good at accepting advice, or help in general," Sam continued as if I hadn't replied at all. She was still using her mom voice because she knew it would make me relent sooner or later. "So it's a good thing that I can't take no for an answer." She inhaled and sat up straight before leveling her determined expression on me again. "I know you're bored out of your mind and feel like you're missing out on all the action happening in the Netherworld. And

I'm more than convinced you're missing Knight like crazy."

"Yes, yes, and yes," I admitted, seeing no way around the fact that Sam was going to insist we have this conversation. The sooner I admitted my own defeat, the sooner I could get back to bouncing the ball against the wall. 'Course, I could always hope that aliens would touch down in Splendor, or a gaggle of angry centaurs would storm through town. If those two options failed, however, my next best hope was that Knight would come back home so we could make stormy, passionate love for the rest of the afternoon and long into the night.

Even though I was bored out of my mind, at the same time, I was also unnaturally antsy. I knew the situation in the Netherworld wasn't all roses and rainbows. Far from it. No, it was basically one big clusterf--k. The reason it had become such an immense, jumbled mess had everything to do with the Head of the Netherworld, who was also my father.

Disclaimer: Even though my father, Melchior O'Neil, and I were genetically related by blood, that's where all similarities ended. My father was a manipulative son of a bitch who had brazenly abused the title as Head of the Netherworld. He was also the top dog of the illegal potions industry, which was basically responsible for distributing illegal street potions from the Netherworld to Earth.

I, meanwhile, was and always had been dedicated to upholding the law and fighting the good fight. As a Regulator for the ANC and, basically, a glorified cop, my sole mission was to make sure the creatures of the Netherworld behaved themselves and didn't cause any problems on the Earthly plane.

Yes it was now common knowledge among humans that creatures such as witches, fairies (that's me!), goblins, werewolves, and vampires existed, but that didn't mean we weren't subject to a harsher set of laws and discrimination, all the same. It was my duty to curtail any wrongdoing by my own in order to ensure that we continued to pave the path to equality, at least where humans were concerned.

So given my job description, you can probably imagine the huge paradox in having a father who was the head honcho of the illegal potions industry. In my defense, though, as soon as I learned that was the case, I severed all familial ties with the man. And that's saying a lot. Since I'd already lost my mother, as far as bloodlines and family went, Melchior was it. Well, that was before I killed him.

"You aren't resentful of Knight that he's over there in the thick of it while you're not?" Sam asked, eyeing me in a way that suggested she imagined the answer was a yes.

"No, I'm not resentful!" I railed at her. Frowning, I let her know in no uncertain terms that I understood the reasons Knight hadn't been around. Because Knight ranked high up in the list of ANC officials, and because he'd been absolutely paramount in helping me take my father out, it made sense that he'd also be a heavyweight when it came to setting up the new world order in the Netherworld. "I'm just disappointed that I can't be a part of it too," I finished, sighing my despondency aloud.

"Well, even though it might not feel like it, you are doing your part, you know?" Sam said, offering me a smile of consolation as she slapped her thighs and looked like she was about to break into song and dance.

"What? By sitting here all day long, throwing a ball at the wall, and getting pep talks from you?"

She shrugged, but that annoying smile was still plastered all over her face. "Well, it's not like we're doing nothing. Last time I checked, we had two weres in custody, as well as a pixie, and we did manage to finally take Rudy down." She paused for a second or two, as if hoping she'd see a smile break across my lips. "That's got to count for something, right?"

Rudy was a goblin who had the bad habit of breaking into houses and dressing up in ladies' undergarments. "Really, Sam? *That's* the best you could do?" I asked. Frowning at her, I shook my head and wondered if this day could get any worse.

"What?" she scoffed, pretending to be offended. "We've been after Rudy for a while!"

"The pantie bandit?"

"My point is: it's not like we're sitting around doing nothing! Even though they might be keeping busier in the Netherworld ..."

"Way busier," I muttered.

"Don't forget that we're keeping the streets of Splendor safe!"

"Right," I argued, feeling my eyebrows knitting together in the middle of my forehead as frustration surged through me. "We're doing a damn good job of protecting Splendor against criminals who want to dress up in bras and panties!" Flustered, I pushed against the desk, the wheels of my chair sending me whizzing backwards, until I rammed into the wall behind me. "While Knight is busy busting the real bad guys, we're keeping Victoria's Secret in business! Good for us!"

"I'm trying here, Dulce," Sam said. Her tone sounded defeated as she shook her head and threw her hands up in the air.

"It's okay," I replied as I tried to smile. Unfortunately, my mouth wasn't ready to comply. "You don't have to do all this, Sam." I stood up and took a deep breath before approaching the window and wondered what was going on in the Netherworld at this very minute. "I understand why I'm here and why Knight is over there. I'm not happy about it; but it is what it is."

Sam didn't say anything, so I turned around to face her. Her attention was settled on the bookcase across the room. Truth be told, this was once Knight's office, before duty summoned him to the Netherworld. Now I was adopting it as my own. I figured if I had to assume the role as Head of the ANC in Splendor, I might as well have the real estate to go along with the title.

"I miss him," she said in a soft voice, directing her attention to a framed photograph of Knight, Sam, me, and one of our old colleagues, Trey. He'd been killed in the Netherworld during the attack on my father. In the picture, Knight's arm was draped around Sam and me, and Sam was hugging Trey who just beamed at the photographer, his round face appearing almost cherubic.

"I know," I said with a sigh that went all the way down to my toes. I couldn't pull my attention away from the photograph even though I tried. In general, I attempted to avoid looking at the picture because it seized me with a depression that took me days to shake.

Even though the photo wasn't shot too long ago, somehow, it seemed like it came from a completely different lifetime. We all looked so happy, so unconcerned with our futures, so completely oblivious. No one had a clue what would happen to Trey, or to all of us.

"There's not a day that goes by that I don't think about him," I admitted.

"He was a good friend to all of us," Sam said, nodding, both of us staring at the picture. It seemed neither of us wanted to break eye contact with the image of a much more innocent time. "And wherever he is now, I'm sure it's a better place."

"I hope so," I whispered. "I really hope so."

The shrill ringing of my cell phone woke me up. I groped for the noisy object on my nightstand, and locating it, I opened my eyes as I wondered who could have been calling me at whatever ungodly hour it was.

"This is Dulcie," I grumbled in a sleep heavy voice, when I didn't recognize the number on the caller ID.

"Dulce?"

It was Knight.

I sat bolt upright and my heartbeat started racing through me as I fought to catch my breath. The darkness of my bedroom suddenly seemed as if it were closing in on me, suffocating me in its velvety blackness. "Is everything okay? Where are you? Are you okay?"

"I'm fine," he answered in a clipped and hurried tone. "I need you to meet me at Headquarters as soon as you can."

"Okay," I answered immediately, wondering what was going on. Preferring to know what I needed to prepare myself for, I asked, "Is there anything I should know before I go down there?"

"No," he answered amidst the sound of other people's voices audible in the background. It sounded like he was in the middle of something. "I don't have time to fill you in right now. Just meet me there?"

"Okay."

"See you in about twenty minutes."

8

"Okay."

"Drive safely," he added in a softer tone before the sounds in the background became considerably louder. I was about to respond, but upon hearing the hollow, droning beep on the other end, I knew Knight had already hung up.

I set the phone back on my bedside table and jumped out of bed, turning on the lamp as I reached for the same pair of jeans I'd worn the previous evening. I followed suit with my sports bra, which was a must seeing as how I'm a natural C cup. I can't run braless without being in a lot of pain.

I pulled on a white, long-sleeved T-shirt, and when I caught my reflection in the mirror, I noticed my elbow-long golden strands were sorely in need of a brush. Since time was of the essence, I grabbed the only baseball cap I owned and secured it on top of my head, hoping it would suffice temporarily. I looked more like a kids' baseball coach than a cop, but c'est la vie!

I fastened my holster around my waist and picked up the Op 6, which sat on my nightstand, beside my cell phone. My Op 6 was a Netherworld-issued gun, and most similar to a 9mm Glock. However, mine was loaded with dragon blood bullets instead of lead— dragon's blood being toxic to any Netherworld creatures. I nestled the gun into the holster and slid my feet into my tennies before running out of the bedroom.

Throwing open the front door to my humble apartment, I hastily locked it behind me before hightailing straight for the ANC-provided black Yukon Denali, which I'd parked right in front of my apartment. I unlocked it and threw myself into the driver's seat, cranking the engine as soon as my butt touched the black leather. Slamming the door shut, I put the SUV in drive, and started for Headquarters, all the while wondering what awaited me there.

ANC Headquarters is a white concrete, two-story building with dark, triangular windows that never fail to remind me of jack-o'-lantern eyes. I live maybe ten minutes from Headquarters, but because I was speeding, I made it in eight. I pulled into the parking lot beside the building and put the Denali into park. Killing the engine, I dropped down to the ground and slammed the door shut behind me before heading for the double doors.

"Hi, Gus," I greeted the night patrolman stationed at the double doors, his hands crossed in front of him and his feet shoulder-width apart. He was huge—as in, he stood eye level with the top of the doors. He was also incredibly broad and solid—one of the primary reasons he made a good watchman. He was an ogre and, as such, not the friendliest of the ANC employees. Not to mention how incredibly hairy he was. Ogres, in general, didn't fare very well with most ladies.

Gus didn't respond, which was usual, but simply nodded as I rushed past him and opened one of the doors. I could smell the weres we had in custody immediately. It wasn't that they smelled particularly bad or offensive, but as a fairy, I have the innate ability to detect every type of creature I come across. And weres always have an earthy, soil, and dirt sort of smell about them.

Hurrying through the lobby and down the narrow hallway that led to our holding cells, I thought I should have probably checked in on our inmates, just to make sure everything was A-OK. As soon as I swiped my hand in front of the small, black security box, which was mounted to the wall beside the iron door, a buzzing sound ensued, followed by a few sparks.

"Ugh, Sam, you have to remember to check your spells from time to time!" I grumbled, shaking my head as I ran my palm in front of the box again. This time, the door slid open like it was supposed to.

"Everything okay?" Wally, one of the guards, asked as soon as he saw me. He was sitting in a chair at the end of the hallway, reading a magazine, and looking as bored as I probably did during most of last week.

"Hi, Wally, yes, everything is good," I answered, flashing the gnome a quick smile.

I walked inside and immediately noticed all three of our prisoners were sound asleep on their cots, and the two weres were happily snoring. The pixie was in one of our smaller containment units, one which was really nothing more than a glorified birdcage suspended from the ceiling. Because pixies are usually less than eight inches tall and they have wings, birdcages serve remarkably well as jail cells.

"Just thought you'd come and visit at two in the morning?" Wally inquired in his deep and gruff voice.

"No, not exactly," I responded with a quick smile. "Knight told me to meet him here." I glanced back up the hall before focusing on Wally again. "Any sign of him?"

"No sign of Mr. Vander," Wally answered as he shook his head, his enormous, flame orange beard swaying beneath him like a sea. He was probably about as tall as me, but very wide and muscular, like most gnomes. Even though he was considered short by anyone's calculation, he was spectacularly fast. Years ago, I actually saw him take down a vampire, which is definitely saying something when it comes to speed.

"Okay, well, thanks," I answered as I turned on my toes, heading for the door again. I checked my phone, realizing that twenty-five minutes had elapsed since Knight and I hung up. "Where are you?" I whispered

11

softly, since my nerves were starting to get the better of me.

No sooner did that thought leave my mind when I heard a popping sound that came from directly behind me. It reminded me of the sound a soda can makes when you snap open the top and the carbon dioxide meets the air. A sort of fizzing noise.

"Hold him steady!" Knight's voice made me whirl around, and nanoseconds later, the air gave birth to him right there in front of me. "Dulcie, get out of the way!" Knight yelled as soon as he saw me. Reaching forward, he gave me a generous push, thrusting me against the wall. If not, I would have found myself smack dab in the middle of a parade of enormous men.

"What?" I asked, in complete bafflement, my mind still reeling over seeing them just materialize from nowhere, as if the air just spat all of them out. It took me a couple of seconds to remember that the only brand of travel between the Netherworld and Earth was via portals, which did exactly that—slipped you through the air and spat you right back out again.

"What's going on?" I demanded, once I regained my voice. My heart continued to pound through me like an SOB, and I was vaguely aware of the weres watching me, wide-eyed. I could hear one of them demanding to know what the hell was going on, not that anyone cared to enlighten him. For my part, I had no idea what was going on. Meanwhile, the pixie was alight and flying through her cage. Seconds later, she landed and started shaking the entire thing as she struggled against the bars, screaming something about her rights.

My eyes moved from Knight's gargantuan body to the man who stood behind him. Sharing Knight's immense height and build, the man was shackled from head to toe, with two other Neanderthal guards on either side of him. His brown hair was long enough to hide his face and obscure his features.

"Throw him in that one," Knight commanded the guard nearest him, nodding toward the unoccupied cell, which lay at the end of the hallway. Wally just stood there, in complete amazement, as if he thought he might have been dreaming the whole thing. I didn't really blame him.

"Wally!" Knight yelled when it seemed the gnome had entered into a trance. The much smaller man immediately came to and nervously nodded as he cleared his throat. He reached for the skeleton key on the chain, which was wrapped around his ample waist, and unlocked the cell. He held it wide as the two men who had custody of the man in chains approached the cell and walked him inside, all of them inching along slowly because the prisoner was bound so heavily.

"Cozy," the man commented as he tilted his head back, ostensibly to get the hair out of his face. His eyes settled on me and widened slightly before a smirk appeared on his mouth. He was handsome—remarkably so. The dimples on either side of his mouth imbued him with a sort of boyish charm that was further accented by the twinkle in his laughing, brown eyes.

"Git used to it," the guard closer to him responded as he forced the shackled man to sit down on the cot. "You're gonna be here for ah long while." The guard then retreated from the cell as Wally locked the prisoner inside.

"I don't suppose one of my guards would happen to be a fairy?" the prisoner asked as he smiled more broadly at me.

I narrowed my eyes in response and threw my hands on my hips, trying to let him know I wasn't

13

impressed. All that did, however, was draw his attention to my bust. When his eyes met mine again, they looked a little less boyish, and a lot more wolfish.

"Ernie and Judah, you keep a good watch over him," Knight commanded the two men who didn't say anything, but simply nodded their compliance before taking up positions on either side of the cell. Wally shrugged and sat back down in his chair, returning to his magazine again as if he couldn't care less that we had visitors. Gnomes were like that though—not exactly the most social race.

"Dulcie," Knight said as he reached for my hand to lead me out of the holding cells and up the hallway. When the iron door slid closed behind us, he glanced down at me and smiled. "Are you okay?" he asked, squeezing my hand.

"Yeah, I'm fine," I answered, half wondering why he was asking me the question in the first place. Then I remembered the whole incident when he'd pushed me out of the way of his entourage. "I'm good," I replied, and my answer reflected the complete truth. Just looking up at this gorgeous man now made me very aware that I was much more than good. Inside, I was beaming.

Physically, Knight is all man, and a very stunning man at that. He's pretty tall—maybe six feet, four inches or so, if I had to guess, but he isn't lanky. His entire body seems to have been sculpted from thick, ropey muscles. His physique is a trait of his race. He's a Loki, a creature that was forged from the fires of Hades and created in Hades's own image, specifically to protect the Netherworld. Lokis are the Netherworld's version of natural-born soldiers.

"I didn't mean to push you so hard," he apologized as he led the way down the hall, toward his office. When we reached it, he opened the door for me and I walked inside. "I was just afraid you'd get trampled."

"That's okay," I answered as I watched him close the door behind him.

He turned on the overhead lights and I held my breath when I saw him bathed in their soft luminescence. He was just as beautiful as I remembered. His black hair was radiant, shining almost blue. It soon became fairly obvious that he was so busy setting up the new Netherworld order that he'd had no time to get a haircut. Long tendrils curled around his ears and reached the base of his neck; and his cheeks and jaw were shadowed with unshaved stubble. The bright lights heightened the angular planes of his face, throwing shadows beneath his cheeks and emphasizing the square lines of his jaw. Best of all were his azure eyes that sparkled from behind his long, black lashes and heavy eyebrows.

"I'm sorry," he semi-whispered. I could only wonder what he was referencing—what he was sorry about. I had no answer though. Like a deer caught in headlights, I was physically unable to pull my attention away from his flawless male beauty. And apparently, I wasn't the only one at a loss for words. Knight stared at me just as intently as I did him. Neither of us spoke or moved. I wasn't even sure I was breathing.

"It's been a long time," he finally said in a deep, throaty voice, interrupting the stillness of the air. "To see you now, I feel like I have to pinch myself to make sure I'm not dreaming," he finished, his eyes never leaving mine.

"It's been too long," I answered, finally feeling able to. The last two months seemed more like two years. Of course, Knight and I talked nearly every day and sent each other photos and the occasional naughty video, but all of those things were trivial consolations when compared to seeing him again in the flesh.

"You are beautiful," he said as his gaze washed over my face, following the tresses of my gold hair down to my breasts. His eyes lingered there for a few seconds before shifting to my waist and legs, and, eventually, returning to my face again. I felt myself shuddering beneath his scrutinizing gaze, a gaze visibly laced with lust. When his eyes found mine again, I felt like he was looking right through me, examining my very essence.

"If you'd given me some advance notice, I would have dressed a little better," I said with a hesitant laugh as I spied my T-shirt, jeans and tennis shoes with disappointment.

"I wouldn't have you any other way," Knight responded, his eyes glued to mine. "I love you just how you are—natural."

"Thank you," I whispered, suddenly feeling nervous beneath his attentive gaze.

"It's your eyes," he replied, studying me as if admiring a famous painting. "It's those damn, emerald eyes of yours that have haunted me for the last couple of months." He shut his own exquisite, sapphire ones as a smirk appeared on his plump lips. "I've practiced incessantly, bringing them to mind every day that we weren't together," he started, and his smile melted my insides.

"What do you mean?" I asked with an anxious little laugh.

"Every time I closed my eyes, I would see yours. I would remember them when you were laughing, or when you were angry, or scared." He opened his eyes again and studied me for a few long seconds. "I promised myself I wouldn't allow the time we spent apart to distort a single memory of you. And it hasn't."

He paused for a few seconds as if he were recalling something.

"I did the same," I admitted with a quick nod. "Every night, although I cheated a little."

"How's that?" he asked with a chuckle.

I shrugged. "Well, I didn't rely on my memory. Instead, I looked at that picture of you that I took a few months ago when you were in my bed and you'd just woken up."

In the picture, Knight was naked but my white duvet covered his lower half. His upper body, though, was bare and visible for any onlooker to appreciate. And he was impossible not to appreciate, with his tan skin that contrasted so deliciously against the crisp white of my bed linens. He was leaning on his elbow, which, in turn, caused his bicep to bulge out like it was trying to imitate the Hulk. But my favorite feature of the photograph was Knight's smile, which never failed to cause my heart to skip a beat.

"The one where my hair looks like I survived a windstorm?"

"Yep, that would be the one," I answered with a wide grin. "It's my favorite picture of you, and I keep it framed above my bed. That way I get to see you before I go to sleep and as soon as I wake up."

He nodded, but it seemed like his thoughts were elsewhere. "Would you like to know which picture of yours is sitting on my bedside table in the hotel?"

"Of course."

His smile broadened. "The one I took of you at Rascal's Curve, when we raced our bikes to the top."

"And I beat you?" I asked, remembering the sunny day as if it were yesterday. We'd taken our motorcycles for a ride and found ourselves at the top of Rascal's Curve, which was an especially twisting and curving canyon.

"I think you beating me is open for interpretation," he said with a quick laugh.

"You can choose to remember it however you want to, but I know the truth."

He didn't respond right away but just looked at me, wearing that smile of his that I found so irresistible. "When we got to the top, you took your helmet off and the wind picked your hair up and blew it over your shoulders just at the exact moment that I snapped a picture of you. In it, you're laughing and your eyes are the greenest I've ever seen them." He paused for a moment or two, and when he spoke again, his voice was a little bit deeper. "Do you know that I can detect your moods just by looking at your eyes?"

I shook my head.

He chuckled as he crossed his large arms over his equally ample chest. "When you're angry, flecks of gold appear in them. When you're sad, they take on a sage sort of green; and then there are those other times, when they become a deep, dark, hunter green."

"And what am I then?" I asked with a smile, taking a few steps toward him as I decided to play his game.

He cocked his head to the side. "It's difficult to say."

"Didn't you just claim that you can read my moods?" I asked with a playful shrug. "Doesn't sound like you're very good at it."

I couldn't help gulping as I focused on his face and saw his eyes were suddenly glowing. It was the surefire sign that his body had selected mine as his mate—that it had made the decision that I was strong enough to bear his seed.

"When your eyes become their darkest, it means you're turned on," he explained.

"What color are they now?" I asked, my voice barely audible.

Knight smiled wider. "The darkest green I've ever seen them."

TWO

I couldn't argue. I was definitely turned on—more turned on than I'd been for a very long time. Two months long, to be exact.

As I watched Knight push up from where he'd been sitting on top of his desk, it felt like millions of insects were busily humming in my stomach, I was so nervous. He started for the door and reached it in a few strides, then locked it. Turning to face me, he smiled languidly and began closing the blinds on all three windows.

"So we're going to do this in your office, huh?" I asked, my voice sounding a little bit shaky since my nerves were going full steam ahead. Even though Knight and I had been together for a while, he never failed to give me butterflies.

"It's been two months," he answered over his shoulder with a shrug. "I don't know about you, but I'm not waiting any longer."

"What if I refuse? I mean, this *is* our workplace," I persisted, pretending to care. The truth was I was just stalling because I enjoyed playing games of cat and mouse with Knight. "What would HR say?"

We had no HR department, so they wouldn't have much to say.

Knight finished closing the third set of blinds and faced me, without saying anything. His smile suggested he knew something I didn't. It was an expression of his that I was very much accustomed to; but, as always, it made my breath catch.

"Last I checked, I was your boss," he replied in a businesslike tone that brooked no arguments. "And that means *you* have to do whatever *I* tell you to do."

"Oh? Is that so?" I asked with an undisguised smile, crossing my arms over my chest to show my disapproval.

"Yes, that's so."

I shook my head as goose bumps started rising all over my body. Knight just had that effect on me. "Last I checked, you were on hiatus for two months, leaving all of the operations for this office in *my* lap, and as such, this office has been my sole responsibility; so I'd say that means I'm the boss of myself." I took a deep breath and audibly exhaled it for added effect. "And, in case you didn't notice, I even took ownership of your office."

"I did notice," Knight answered with a frown. He picked up a pink-haired troll doll from my collection of twelve with which I'd adorned the top of his desk. He briefly examined the miniature with obvious distaste before replacing it beside its blue-haired brother. Then he turned around with a very determined scowl.

"Trolls, Dulce? Really?"

"Toys R Us was fresh out of Lokis, sorry," I answered with a shrug.

"Well, now that I've resumed my role as head of this office, and my role as *your boss*, I order you to remove all these obnoxious creatures at once," he announced boldly.

I frowned and shook my head as I offered him an expression of consolation. "I hate to break the news to you, buddy, but seeing as how I've been managing myself as well as this office for the last couple of months, you're going to have to convince me that you're my boss."

"Is that so?"

I nodded. "And, just so you know, convincing me isn't going to be easy," I finished with an apologetic shrug.

"Going on hiatus doesn't mean I stopped being your boss," he pointed out.

He wore a lofty expression as he leaned his exquisite ass against the edge of the desk while regarding me with visible amusement. Even though I wanted nothing more than to attack him right there, I swallowed my enthusiasm and forced myself to pay attention to our little game of playful seduction.

"Hmm," I started, drumming my fingers against my lips. "A salient point," I continued in my best lawyer-ese. "But even if I played the role of devil's advocate and agreed with you, I would have to warn you that you still have a small problem on your hands."

"I do? How's that?"

I pretended to be deep in thought for the next few seconds to avoid answering. I'd never been much of an actress, but this seemed like a good way to prolong the theatrics. "Well, since you *have* been gone for soooo long, and I acted as the boss around here, I've sort of let all that power go to my head."

"You don't say," he responded with a chuckle. Crossing one ankle over the other, he observed me with a smile. The man had no business being so damn sexy. It should have been illegal. Holy Hades, for all I knew, maybe in some states, it was.

"It's unfortunate, but yes," I replied, shaking my head like the whole thing was a shameful tragedy. "I'm just not sure I can follow anybody's rules anymore. I mean, I'm much more partial to following my own."

Knight nodded as he exhaled deeply and rubbed the back of his neck. Then he focused on his feet. "That creates quite the conundrum then," he admitted with a quick glance at me. His eyes seemed to dance as a mischievous smile overtook his mouth. "But I'm sure I can rectify the situation. If I'm good at anything, it's reschooling any employees who dare to go rogue."

I shook my head, trying to stifle my smile, while staying in character. Even though I was more than looking forward to our sexual reunion, which certainly hovered on the horizon, I had to admit our little game possessed its own level of delicious foreplay.

"Yeah, well, I'm not ready to hand over the power, or the control; not just yet." I sighed as I continued to shake my head. "You're going to find yourself with quite a fight on your hands."

"Luckily for you, I'm a lover ... and a fighter," Knight answered with a hearty chuckle.

Standing up, he began approaching me. When he was maybe a foot away, he stopped walking. I had to restrain myself from closing my eyes and inhaling as deeply as I could. I wanted nothing more than to fill myself with his clean, masculine scent. Instead, I held my ground and continued our charade, truthfully loving every minute of it.

I watched him reach for me and grasp my upper arms in his large hands. A shiver of nervous anticipation raced through me, causing my breath to catch. I could already feel something beginning to blossom deep down in my core. Something that felt like an intense stinging blended with the thrill of anticipation.

"I won't give in easily," I warned him with a smile.

"I wouldn't expect otherwise, my little hellcat." He stared down at me for a few seconds, his eyes alight with passion. "Especially now that you're going AWOL."

I shook my head and made a tsking sort of noise to let him know he was way off base. "No, Knightley, I'm not *going* AWOL, I've already *gone* AWOL."

"Ah, so it's progressed to that stage, has it?" I didn't respond as I watched his eyes glow even more brightly before another smile curled his full lips.

"It has," I answered resolutely. "Sounds like you've got a long, difficult road ahead of you, Knightley, my man."

"That's Officer Vander to you," he corrected me.

Then he jerked me forward, and none too gently. I brought my hands up against his chest to keep my face from slamming into him. When I caught my breath, I looked up and instantly lost myself in the stunning cerulean blue of his eyes. Less than three inches of air separated us, but that was dwindling fast, owing to my increased respiration.

Boiling with exhilaration, I couldn't help but notice how Knight dwarfed me with his enormous body. His impressive size was one of the things that thrilled me the most about him. The extreme difference in our heights and builds made me feel so feminine, so small and fragile and it was an observation that electrified me all the way to my core. As exhilarating as it was, it was also a weird thought, especially to me. I was generally known as the feisty, independent woman who could always take care of herself. Ordinarily, my code of law was kicking asses and taking names. Sometimes, though, I had to admit that I enjoyed the role of submissive to this deliciously dominant alpha male.

Okay, well, let's say, I enjoyed *playing* the role of *sexually* submissive. In general, "submissive" wasn't a word that anyone would use to characterize me. And in my mind that was definitely a good thing.

"Excuse me ...," I said with a small laugh. "Officer ... Knight."

He narrowed his eyes in mock offense and I was suddenly overwhelmed by the need to feel his lips on mine. I was dying to taste him, to experience the delight of his tongue as it entered my mouth. The need inside me was growing to such an extent that it soon became an all-out conflagration, a burning desire that pleaded for relief.

"I won't tolerate insolence," he whispered before releasing my right arm. His hold on my left arm tightened; and seconds later, I felt the sharp smack of his palm hitting my right butt cheek. All I was aware of was my sharp intake of breath as he unleashed his hand on my other cheek. The sting was momentary, and far outweighed by my own burning desire, which was mounting exponentially inside me.

"Am I supposed to apologize?" I asked. My voice was a little breathy because I wanted nothing more than for him to smack my ass again.

"You're supposed to show some respect for your superiors," he answered. He started massaging both of my cheeks, as if he felt bad for inflicting even the slightest amount of pain on them. Truth be told, I'd enjoyed every second of it.

"And if I refuse?"

He chuckled as he gripped my right cheek more tightly. "Then you must endure even more punishment."

"Hmm," I replied. Rising up onto my tiptoes, I whispered into his ear, "What if the punishment is exactly what I'm after? Should I be punished even harder?"

"You're incorrigible," he chuckled, but seconds later, he lifted me up. I wrapped my legs around him and he sat me down on top of the desk. Wedging his body between my legs, he said, "You have no idea how much I've missed you." His hot breath on my neck preceded a series of kisses that made my insides feel like they were melting.

"I'm sure I have a pretty good idea," I answered and reached for his erection, which was already straining for release from his pants. Maybe it was because of Knight's rank, or because he was a detective, but he didn't have to wear a uniform. He never had. And although I loved the way he dressed, at that moment I would have given just about anything to see his beautiful body clad in sexy, police-issue pants.

"Don't degrade what I'm trying to say by making it all about sex," he chided me. He pulled away and gripped my chin, forcing me to look him right in the eyes. "Our sex life is unparalleled, and of course I've missed it, but that's not what I was talking about."

"Okay, Mr. Serious."

"I *am* being serious," he continued, his expression emphasizing the point. "I missed *you*, Dulcie."

"Point taken," I said with a resolute nod. "Now let's get back to the more fun stuff."

He shook his head and a sweet smile appeared on his lips. "Okay. But I want to make sure you know that I don't think of you as just a hot piece of ass," he explained before quirking a brow at me.

"Hmm, what if I can't say the same about you?"

Feigning offense, he effortlessly lifted me off the desk and then took a seat on it. He put me on my feet and gripped me around my middle, forcing me to bend over his knees. With one arm across my back, he held me in place. Meanwhile his other hand gave me a healthy swat right across my backside.

"So I'm just a piece of meat to you, am I?" he asked before unleashing his palm against my ass again.

"You always valued truth above all else in our relationship, right?" I ground out, smiling up at him as non-apologetically as I could.

He didn't respond as he wound his arm back and unfurled it against my butt again, this time a little bit harder. The smack made my entire body bounce, so I dug my fingernails into his thighs.

"You could always take back what you said, you know, and admit I'm your boss," he announced, cocking his head to the side as he spoke. "I *am* a reasonable man."

"And why would I do that?" I inquired, shaking my head. "Especially when my punishment was just starting to get really good."

"Have it your way," Knight shrugged as he smacked me again. Another four, and I decided I'd had enough. My butt was stinging, and then some.

"Okay, okay," I said, anxious to surrender. "I give up! You win!"

"Say it," he replied, straight-lipped. With a backwards glance, I noticed he held his hand up, as if poised to lay it on me if my answer displeased him.

"Say what?"

"Really?" he asked, shaking his head and frowning. "You don't recall the conversation we were just having?"

I smiled as apologetically as I could. "To be completely honest, I can't remember anything before you started in on me. Forgive me; but every other thought I had just sort of blanched altogether from my mind."

"Unbelievable," he grumbled, shaking his head again and frowning directly at me. I smiled even more broadly. "I was telling you how much I missed you," he started.

"Ah!" I interrupted, grinning as widely as I could. "I missed you too!"

With a loud laugh, he lifted me off his knees and set me down on the desktop again, right beside him. I couldn't help noticing how his hands lingered around my waist. We looked at each other for a few seconds, neither of us saying anything, as both of our smiles disappeared.

"I love you, Dulcie O'Neil," Knight whispered.

"I love you, Knightley Vander," I whispered back before running my hands up his arms.

I loved feeling the swells of his forearms and biceps. But as much as I appreciated Knight's body, it was his face that always held me spellbound. Most specifically, his eyes. They were kind, loyal, strong, and determined. In the depths of his irises, though, there was something else. Something deep and something dark. Knight hadn't exactly led an easy life. I could read the magnitude of his struggles in the depths of his eyes, as well as the fact that he was a survivor. Right now, however, the vastness of his love for me dominated his eyes and his expression in general.

"So are you going to kiss me, or what?" I demanded. It felt like I was on the precipice of losing myself in the awe-inspiring sapphire of his gaze. And that, although nice, wasn't my main goal at the moment.

He chuckled and bent his head down before covering my lips with his very full ones. I wrapped my arms around his neck, pulling him closer when his tongue invaded my mouth. I couldn't seem to catch my breath. A deep ache started to build from inside me. My tongue met his tongue with territorial fierceness. I wanted to taste him; I needed it badly. Our tongues mated while I wrapped my legs around his middle and pushed my abdomen onto his straining erection. He had to put both of his palms flat on the desk so we wouldn't topple over. Once he did, I managed to pull myself against him even harder, conveying how badly I desired him.

Over the last two months, I'd imagined our reunion numerous times. And I'd always pictured Knight taking me slowly, gently making love to me. Now? The idea of going slow and gentle left everything to be desired. Now my need was almost frantic in its demand to be satiated. I couldn't wait a second longer. I reached down and gripped his throbbing erection with both hands, rubbing it up and down on top of his pants. Knight didn't stop kissing me, but leaned closer and his tongue delved inside my mouth more deeply.

I couldn't wait to unzip his pants. As soon as I did, I slipped his hard penis through the hole in his boxers. He broke away from me and glanced down briefly. He was totally out in the open and such a completely glorious sight to behold.

"Dulcie," he started in a disappointed tone. "Don't rush. Let me taste you."

"No," I nearly interrupted him. "I need to feel you inside me. Right now."

He studied me for a few seconds. Then his expression changed to one of sudden impatience, probably mirroring my own. Sliding off his pants, he dropped them to the floor; then his boxers followed. He snatched my ball cap and pulled it off my head, letting it fall onto the desk beside me. His eyes never strayed from mine as he expertly unbuttoned my jeans before unzipping them and pulling them down my thighs. I decided to help him out by pulling my shirt over my head until I was only clad in my bra and panties. But then remembering my sports bra wasn't exactly the sexiest, I wasted no time in removing it, too.

Knight's eyes immediately fastened onto my naked breasts. He leaned down and took my left nipple between his teeth. I dropped my head back and arched up against him when he rolled the sensitive nub against his tongue. When his fingers began rubbing the outside of my panties, I couldn't help moaning loudly.

"Please, Knight," I whispered, too eager to drag this out any longer than we needed to. I ached to have him thrusting inside me. I needed to feel him; I needed us to reunite as one.

His response was a chuckle as he slid my panties to the side and ran his index finger up and down my opening. I nearly jumped right out of my skin.

"Please," I whispered again, thrusting my pelvis toward him for easier access, but he just pulled his erection away from me.

"Please what?" he asked as I opened my eyes and glared at him.

"Knight, I can't wait any longer," I pleaded, my voice sounding strained. "I need to feel you inside me right now."

"I was expecting a fight," he replied with a wide smile. "Didn't you promise me one?"

"Really?" I asked, sarcastically. "How about this—if you don't bury yourself inside me in two seconds, you're going to have the fight of your life!"

He didn't say anything but just continued to smile down at me, the look of seduction in his eyes. I met his gaze with as much impudence as I could muster. When he didn't make any motion to comply with my demand, I spread my legs wider. Lifting my torso up to his, I practically performed a charade of what I wanted, and in no uncertain terms. He continued to stare down at me, although he positioned himself closer to my entrance. When I felt the head of his penis

30

bobbing against me, I tried to push myself down against it, to force him inside me, but again, he retreated.

"Repeat after me," he said. "You're my boss and I answer to you."

I opened my eyes and then narrowed them at him and replied, "Never."

He cocked his head to the side and pulled away from me. The stark coldness of the air on my very hot lady parts was almost enough to bring tears to my eyes.

"Two can play this game, my dear," he said in a victorious tone. "Now, repeat after me 'I, Dulcie O'Neil, do fully submit to my boss, Knightley Vander, who, I now declare, has complete authority over me.'"

"You're really going to force this issue right now?" I asked in disbelief. I hated knowing I would probably have to give in but there was no way I could wait any longer. My body was in a state of dire need and it was demanding instant gratification.

"In short, yes."

"Oh my God," I grumbled with a deep breath and readied myself to hand him the victory. "I, Dulcie O'Neil, do fully submit to Knightley …"

"No, you missed a part," he interrupted with a shake of his head. "You're supposed to say 'to my boss, Knightley Vander," he finished, giving me an expression that said I had better get it right.

"Ugh," I muttered, shaking my head. "… Do fully submit to my boss, Knightley Vander, who, I now declare, has complete control …"

"Authority," he corrected me.

"Authority over me," I finished with a perturbed scowl. "There, you won! Satisfied?"

He pushed the head of his penis over my most sensitive place, causing me to arch back before a moan escaped my mouth. Any words of frustration or resistance were instantly forgotten.

"No, I'm not satisfied yet," he announced before extracting himself from me again.

"What?" I scolded him, opening my eyes, and finding him smiling happily at me. "You're unbelievable!"

"There's more; I want to hear more from you," he said with a shrug. "Repeat after me: 'I, Dulcie O'Neil, recognize Knightley Vander as my boss, and from here on out, I will follow all of his orders without pause or question.'"

"I have half a mind to get my vibrator."

"That would require a trip home, and I think we both known that isn't going to happen," he answered in a calm tone. He already knew he'd won. "So, get to it."

I inhaled deeply, narrowing my eyes at him all the while. "I, Dulcie O'Neil," I started before swallowing my breath as soon as I felt him rubbing his throbbing erection against my opening again.

"Go on," he encouraged me.

"I," I started again, trying to pay attention to what was coming out of my mouth. "I, Dulcie O'Neil, recognize Knightley Vander as my boss," I quoted, spitting the words out. In response, Knight thrust the head of his erection inside me as I screamed out and arched against him. It was all I could do to moan the rest of the words.

Seconds later, he pulled out again. "Continue!" he commanded me.

"And I will follow all your orders!" I yelled out, arching against him again as soon as he pushed himself fully inside me. I gripped his back, digging my fingernails into his tan skin as he pumped inside me a few times.

"And?" he persisted in a deep, gravelly voice.

"Without pause or question!" I regurgitated as he gripped my waist with both of his hands. He lifted me so he could thrust inside me even more deeply. I threw my head back and wrapped my legs around his middle as tightly as I could. He pulled out and then pushed into me, each of us moaning in turn.

Without any warning, he suddenly pulled up. Our lower halves were still joined as he pushed me down against the desk, holding me there. When I looked up at him in question, his eyes were glowing.

"You are mine," he announced as he stared down at me. He withdrew and then began pushing inside me gently.

"And you are mine," I reiterated obediently. I loved seeing and hearing that possessive, brutal side of him; it was so primitive and bestial. This was the animal side of Knight that made me unable to catch my breath.

"I will always be yours," he answered while lifting my legs above his shoulders and burying himself inside me as deeply as he could.

"So who is the guy now taking up one of our prison cells?" I asked Knight as I lay against him, naked in his bed.

After having sex in his office, we both hurriedly dressed and hightailed it back to his lavish townhouse. I wasn't sure whether or not we'd spend the night together, owing to his duties in the Netherworld, so I was thrilled when we did.

"That charming example of a law-abiding citizen is Jax Rochefort," Knight answered, his lips in a tight line.

"Jax Rochefort," I repeated, shaking my head since the name meant nothing to me.

"He's been a perpetual thorn in my side for at least the last seven years," Knight added as he glanced down at me. He busily twirled a tendril of my hair between his fingers and pulled me closer so he could kiss me on the forehead. "And now he's back to being a pain in my ass again."

"If he's behind bars," I started, shaking my head, "how much of a pain in your ass can he really be?"

Knight raised his brows at me, suggesting, *you don't know what you're talking about.* "Behind bars or not, Jax was, and continues to be, a pain in my ass," he ground out. "And he's not the only one. All the competing factions of potions smugglers have been vying for power since we deposed your father."

"What do you mean?"

Knight shrugged again. "Just because the ANC announced Caressa was the new Head of the Netherworld, doesn't mean everyone likes it, or complies with it." He cleared his throat. "In fact, there is plenty of opposition."

Caressa Brandenburg was the highest ranking official in the ANC, aside from my father. When Knight and I removed my father from office, it only made sense that Caressa should replace him as Head of the Netherworld. I supported this approach because Caressa was honest and good and most of all, she was strong. But now, I had to wonder if she were strong enough.

"So these potions rings are trying to put their own guys in?" I asked for verification.

Knight nodded. "But they aren't too smart about it."

"What do you mean?"

"They rely on strength in numbers—there are so many of them, they nearly outnumber us. But the main problem for them is they can't get their shit together long enough to unite forces against us."

"Maybe it's just a matter of time before they do?"

Knight cocked his head to the side as he nodded. "That's what we're worried about. The day that happens, we could have a serious fight on our hands."

"So how does Jax figure into this? Was he trying to usurp power?"

"No," Knight answered as he shook his head. He placed one of the pillows behind him so he could sit up against the headboard more comfortably. "I'm not sure how he fits in, to be honest."

"Okay," I said doubtfully, wondering whether or not he had anything more to add to his statement. "Soooo, how did you catch him?"

"I wouldn't say we caught him."

I leaned up onto one elbow and studied him quizzically. "Well, he's in one of our jail cells at this very moment, so I'd say you caught him."

"It's more correct to say that Jax caught us," Knight amended. "He turned himself in."

"Why would he do that?"

"Exactly," Knight answered before tapping his index finger on the tip of my nose, as if to say I'd hit it right on the nose. "That's the exact question I've been asking myself and, more importantly, Jax."

"And?"

"And nothing," he replied with a sigh, shaking his head. In general, Knight didn't like it when his questions outnumbered his answers.

"He hasn't told you anything?"

"Well, he hasn't told me anything I believe, anyway," Knight admitted with a shrug.

Why do *you* think he turned himself in?"

"He said he wanted to leave the thug life and start a new life and needed protection, yadda yadda yadda."

"And you don't believe that?"

"Of course not!" he responded with snort of disbelief. "Why should I?"

It was my turn to shrug. "Maybe he's telling the truth? Is it so inconceivable to believe some of these guys might want to start over and leave their old lives behind them?"

Knight shook his head. "With someone else, I might buy it, but as it pertains to Jax Rochefort, I can't and I won't."

I nodded, even though I wasn't sure what to make of it. "So why did you come all the way to Splendor to lock him up? The Netherworld prisons weren't secure enough?"

Knight shook his head. "Jax is too high profile. It would be impossible to hide him. And he was very up front about all the hits he knows are out on him. Regardless of what I might think, we have to take him seriously."

"If he has a hit out on him, or multiple hits, that has to mean he spilled information to you, right?"

Knight nodded. "Yes, of course. But whether or not that information is valid is another question. So far, we have yet to validate anything that comes out of his mouth."

"So you think he's lying?"

"We shall see." He smiled at me and secured the tendril of hair he'd been playing with behind my ear. "In the meantime, we have to take any threats to his safety seriously. That's why I decided to bring him to Splendor. It won't be as easy to find him here as in the Netherworld."

I just nodded, unsure how to interpret the information. "For how long?"

Knight shrugged. "Not sure yet. Maybe a couple of days."

I just nodded as I remembered the large man with the dimpled smile who was now calling our jail home. "So I got the feeling that Jax is a Loki like you?"

"I thought you weren't able to detect my species?" Knight replied with a raised eyebrow of suspicion aimed at me.

Cocking my head to the side, I stared at his well-defined pecs for a few seconds before I started snaking my fingers down his chest. "I can't detect your species," I admitted finally. "But based on my inability to place him, I figured that meant he was a Loki, just like you. That and you guys look like you could be twins, well bodily anyway," I glanced back up at him and smiled to say I was proud of myself and my powers of deduction.

"Twins?" he asked with a frown. "Should I take that to mean you thought he was good looking?"

I shrugged, feeling my smile widening because I suddenly wanted nothing more than to stoke the fires of his jealousy. "Well, yeah," I started. "I mean, come on, he's obviously a handsome guy."

"Oh, really?"

"Yeah, really."

"Uh huh," he continued as he reached over and gripping me around my middle, started tickling my sides. "I'd love to know how hot you think he is."

"I," I started amid giggles as I fought to emancipate myself. "I...think...he's...really....hot!"

"Tell me more!" he responded with a chuckle as he released my sides and gripped my feet.

"No!" I yelled at him. "Not my feet! They're way too ticklish." But he didn't release me right away. "Come on, Knight, I'm being serious. Not my feet!"

"So am I," he answered with a frown as he perched his fingers over the bottoms of my feet threateningly. "Tell me how hot Jax is again."

"He's not as hot as you are," I replied immediately.

"Getting better," he said with a grin as he ran his index finger down the center of my foot and caused me to wiggle against him in an attempt to free myself.

"He's nowhere near as hot as you are!" I continued, feeling like I was begging for my life. But he must not have been satisfied with my response because he continued to tease me with his finger. "You're the hottest guy I've ever seen!" I said with another laugh. "No one can compare to you!"

Knight smiled more broadly at me as he released my foot and I breathed out a sigh of relief. Then he gripped me by the arms and pulled me into the warmth of his chest, wrapping his arms around me while I snuggled against him.

"How do you know Jax?" I asked.

"He was in my training class way back when."

"So you know each other pretty well?"

"We used to," he corrected me. "Then, somewhere along the line, he got mixed up with the wrong crowd. I didn't hear from him for a good few years—probably while he was making a name for himself in the street potions business."

I nodded, but lacking any more to say on that topic, I dropped it. "When do you have to go back?" I asked, although I was dreading his answer. It felt so natural and right to have his huge, warm body pressed up against mine. Having him here with me now made me wonder how I'd managed to make it through all of those nights by myself.

"In the morning," he answered with a heartfelt sigh.

"I figured." I was unable to mask the disappointment in my tone and, instead, focused my attention on the huge scar that bisected half his chest. It was from a tangle with a werewolf that had happened long before I'd ever met him.

"I'm sorry, Dulce," he started. "Once everything over there calms down, I'll be able to come back here permanently. It'll probably be no more than a couple of months."

"I know," I said quickly, not wanting to sound like a nagging girlfriend. "I'm not upset. I know how busy you are and how important this is for all of us." I glanced up at him and smiled. "Don't worry about me, okay?"

"Of course I worry about you, Dulce," he answered and pulled me in even closer. "There isn't a day that goes by when you aren't uppermost on my mind." He exhaled deeply. "But this is just one of those things that we both have to deal with."

"I know," I said with a slight smile to tell him he didn't have to explain anything further.

"I appreciate your patience more than you know," he continued. "And I want nothing more than to get back here as quickly as I can. You must realize that."

"I do," I said, resting my head against his chest and inhaling as deeply as I could. Then, with a yawn, I unwittingly closed my eyes, feeling so at home in his large arms.

THREE

The next morning wasn't easy for me.

I woke up, and immediately rolled over, hoping to find Knight's warm body right beside me. Instead, I found nothing but empty space, only the stark whiteness of the sheets greeting me. Yep, Knight was already gone.

I sighed my despondency and tried to ignore the boulder that was already taking shape in the pit of my stomach. How long would I have to wait now until I saw him again? Another two months? Three? Four? Six?

I shook my head as I dreaded the upcoming days and weeks and possible months that I'd have to endure alone. I wasn't even sure how I'd managed to make it through the last two months. In a way, seeing him made his absence hurt even more; the blatant vacancy I felt without him made things exponentially worse.

Dulcie, stop acting like a lovesick dumbass! I scolded myself. *Your life was fine before Knight came into it, and it will be fine until you see him again. Stop feeling sorry for yourself! Get a move on! You've got a full day ahead of you!*

I sat up and noticed a folded piece of paper on Knight's pillow. I reached for it and, unfolding it, read:

Dulce, I'm sorry I had to leave so early—Caressa texted me with an emergency meeting. I didn't want to wake you when you were sleeping like an angel. Be back as soon as I can. I love you. –K.

I folded it in half again and clutched it to my chest, feeling a smile breaking out on my face.

"I love you too, Knight," I said out loud.

I was half hoping that one of his never ending Loki skills might include the ability to hear his girlfriend's voice despite being in another dimension. But when I received no response, I figured that was one trait that wasn't in his arsenal. Bummer.

Even though the note from Knight warmed my spirits a little bit, it was still outweighed by the emptiness that claimed me as soon as I realized Knight was gone. I exhaled and forced myself to get up. Then I threw on a pair of tan cargo pants and an old Duran Duran T-shirt that was nearly threadbare, I'd washed it so many times. Even though I was headed to Headquarters, I didn't feel like dressing the part. That was another perk to being the boss—wearing what I wanted.

But then thoughts of Headquarters led to thoughts of Knight and what had happened the last time I'd been inside his office and I started getting depressed all over again. As soon as my pity party started again, I nipped the feelings right in the bud, forcing them right out of my head. Depressing thoughts had no place in my life. I had a job to do—get to Headquarters and find out as much as I could about this Jax character.

So now, you're basically no more than a glorified babysitter. That miserable voice, the one that always states the obvious, started in my head again.

I've got a job to do and that's the end of it, I snapped back with as much authority as I could muster. I was pleased to find that my alternate self had no come back.

After I got dressed, I made Knight's bed before running/walking through the hallway that led to the front door. The faster I left his home, the easier it would be to focus on other things. Once I was outside, I breathed a sigh of relief. Then locking his front door, I banished the persistent doubt of when I'd be inside his townhouse again to the darkest recesses of my mind. I could only hope it would be sometime in the very near future.

After I left Knight's place, I drove back to my crappy, little apartment. I had to feed my dog, Blue, as well as take him for a walk. Yes, I wasn't supposed to have a dog; my apartment wasn't exactly dog friendly. But luckily for me, being on the ground floor, I actually had a small yard, never mind it was all cement. And even more lucky for me, I was a fairy which meant I was able to magick special wards around the place so my nosy neighbors and my landlord had no clue I was breaking any tenant rules.

After I fed Blue and took him for a much-needed walk, I was ready to head into the office so I could interrogate our newest prisoner. But as soon as Blue was back in his yard, he became very aware that I was on my way out again. He started whining and pawing at the slider screen, looking completely depressed and pathetic.

"Seriously, dude?" I asked as he whined and stared at me, cocking his head to the side. "Come on, Blue, don't make that face!" After another few seconds, I was jelly. "Ugh!" I said in exasperation, throwing my hands in the air and starting for the slider door. I was no more than a pushover where the yellow Labrador was concerned. "You can come with me to work today, but only if you're on your best behavior!" I warned him. I opened the door and let him inside the house again. He simply looked up at me with those bright brown eyes before trotting happily to the front door, where he retrieved his leash from the doorknob. I clipped it to his collar and we headed out for the Denali.

After securing him into his doggie seat belt in the backseat, I rolled the window down so he could poke his head out, and we were off. It took me a little bit longer than ten minutes to make it to Headquarters because I didn't drive as quickly, or as recklessly, when Blue was in the car. Maybe it was just my maternal instincts coming out ... Well, for my dog anyway.

"Remember our deal, Blue," I said as I parked the Denali outside Headquarters. "You need to be a good boy today, got it? Otherwise, Mommy can't bring you back to work with her again."

Blue just looked up at me innocently while his tail wreaked havoc on the interior of the car, leaving coarse, yellow hairs all over the black leather upholstery. I frowned and figured I'd have to get the Denali washed sooner rather than later.

I unbuckled Blue and got him out of the car; then we trotted up to the front doors and allowed ourselves inside. Elsie, the receptionist, nearly jumped out of her seat when she saw us.

"Blue!" she called out before immediately coming around to the front of her desk. She pushed her thick, black glasses back onto her long, narrow nose, and crouched down on her knees. Enveloping Blue in a huge hug, she didn't appear to mind at all when he whipped her with his thick, wagging tail. "I missed you, boy!" she said in her unnaturally high-pitched voice. She reached behind her where she kept doggie treats in a jar on top of her desk. Popping off the top and selecting one, she handed it to the very appreciative dog.

"Good morning to you too, Elsie," I said, pretending to be offended.

"Oh, hi, Dulce," she answered as she glanced up at me for a second or so with a quick smile. "Sorry, I just get very excited whenever I get to see your adorable little boy!" The eardrum-splitting, high pitch of her voice steadily increased. I briefly worried all the glass in the office might shatter and come crashing down around us.

"Else, if you aren't busy this morning, would you mind dog sitting?" I asked. I was grateful, for once, that Knight wasn't around; because this never would have flown with him. Knight wasn't exactly the *sure!-you-can-bring-your-dog-to-work* kind of boss. Especially when said dog was given to me by my previous boss who also happened to be my ex love interest.

"No problem!" Elsie almost sang, reaching for Blue's leash, which I eagerly handed to her.

"Thanks, Else," I called over my shoulder as I started down the hallway. Thoughts of my ex-boss, Quillan, were already occupying my mind.

Even though Quill and I were now good friends, there was a time in the not-so-distant past when I'd wished he and I could have been something else, something more. And he'd felt the same. Then, a cyclone, who went by the name of Knight Vander, stormed into my life. After him, no other men could compare.

I later learned that Quill had been serving as my father's right-hand man all along, unbeknownst to me. In the end, Quill, however, did come clean about all of it. He even sided against my father; but as far as I was concerned, the damage was already done. Even if Knight hadn't been in the picture, I could never have given myself to Quill fully, not after knowing his past. But that was all a moot point now. Both Quill and I had found people who made us happy. Now, we were no longer in each other's sights.

As with Knight, I hadn't seen Quill in a couple of months eother. He was also stationed in the Netherworld, helping to set up the new order. And he and Knight weren't the only ones. Christina Sabbiondo, Knight's second in command, and also Quill's girlfriend, was actively planning for the new Netherworld, along with my very good friend, Dia Robinson.

Dia had been the head of the ANC in Moon, here on the Earthly plane, before business in the Netherworld drew her there. I was the only one, well, Sam and I, were the only ones stuck here with not a hell of a lot to do and all day to do it in.

Not that I was complaining ...

"Morning, Sam!" I called out as I passed by her desk. I aimed straight for the break room, where I could already smell a fresh pot of coffee brewing. Coffee was the one benefit of the morning that compensated for the fact that I was awake.

"Morning, Dulce," Sam said as she came up behind me. I could hear her heels clicking on the tiles in the break room. I never understood why Sam bothered with heels; she was already so damn tall. Not to mention how uncomfortable heels could be. I always opted for tennis shoes because in my line of work, they could mean the difference between life and death. If you aren't able to run, you're as good as dead ...

"I brought Blue with me to work today," I said as I rescued my mug from the sink.

"I saw that," Sam responded. She watched me inspect the mug to make sure whatever was previously living in the bottom of it wasn't life-threatening. But growing ever more suspicious of the gunk in the bottom, I decided to wash it.

"Good thing Knight isn't here," Sam continued. "I doubt he'd be too happy to see Blue."

"Yeah, I was thinking the same thing," I agreed before rinsing out the suds in the mug and drying it. The coffee was ready so I poured myself a cup and gave my best friend a broad smile as I added cream and sugar until the coffee was the color of caramel. "How are you?" I asked.

"Probably not as good as you are," she answered with a quick smile and a knowing expression. "I heard Knight came into town last night?"

I smiled more broadly at the memory of our evening. "Yes, he did."

"No wonder you look like a giddy schoolgirl this morning."

"Oh, stop!" I said, waving her away with an embarrassed smile, which I then hid behind my mug as I attempted to take a sip of the hot coffee. At her insistent grin, I realized there was something she wasn't telling me. "Okay, out with it! What's that smile all about?"

"You aren't the only one who is giddy this morning," she announced.

"Really?" I asked as I took another sip of coffee. "And who is the very lucky man?"

A blush stole across her cheeks as she leaned against the refrigerator and crossed her arms against her chest. "His name is Jordan and he's this cop I met at Starbucks a week or so ago."

"Wow, look at you! And what is he?"

"He's human," she said with a sigh that belied her disappointment. I immediately felt my shackles rise because I'd had a long relationship with a human once and it hadn't led anywhere good. In fact, I regretted it completely.

"Does he know you're a witch?" I asked.

She frowned and then shook her head, her expression one of concern. "Not exactly."

"Be careful, Sam," I said as I inhaled deeply. "Remember my whole situation with Jack, the shithead. You know not all humans accept us."

"I know," she answered immediately. "And it's not like I think I'll ever see him again. I mean, he's cute and what not, but I wouldn't be that bummed out if he didn't call me again."

"You sure?" I asked as I eyed her, trying to decipher if she was being honest with me, well, and herself, for that matter.

"Yeah, I'm fine," she insisted and then shrugged. "Sometimes a girl just has to get a little bit of action, you know? I mean, I don't want my fun parts to shrink up and fall off due to disuse."

I laughed and nodded. "Amen to that!"

"Speaking of, was your reunion everything you hoped it would be?" she asked. Her expression told me she wanted to hear all of the juicy details.

"Everything and more," I answered instantly. Then, with a sigh, I remembered the part about waking up alone this morning. "And then he had to go back to the Netherworld."

"He'll be back, Dulce, you know that," Sam said in her best understanding voice. When it came to sympathy, Sam could have written volumes.

"I know, but that doesn't make it any less difficult." Sam nodded and I could tell she was searching for another subject to lighten my mood.

Luckily for her, I was ready to help her. "Listen, Sam, I can't really talk at the moment because the reason Knight came by last night was to drop off a very high-profile prisoner who will be spending some time with us." Then I remembered why Knight brought Jax to Splendor rather than letting him do his time in a Netherworld prison. "Oh, and keep this all on the DL because it's very hush-hush," I added, knowing that I could trust Sam to keep any and all information to herself.

"I'll zip my lips," she said, pretending to do just that.

"Thanks," I answered with a hurried smile as I walked past her, being careful not to spill my coffee on the way. "Anyway, I've gotta go find out what this guy's story is," I said with a quick, apologetic smile. "But let's catch up over lunch today? I'm dying to get all the juicy information about your cop."

"Sure thing," Sam said while nodding. "Oh, and Dulce?"

I stopped walking, turning to face her again. "Yeah?"

"Be careful, okay?"

I smiled at her warmly and nodded, feeling suddenly extra grateful that she was such a good friend. She was definitely one-of-a-kind. "I will," I said as I turned back around, wondering what type of person Jax Rochefort could be.

One thing I could say about Jax was that he was definitely a Loki. Even though I wouldn't have said he looked like Knight, they both shared similar physical features. Jax was about as tall as Knight and maybe even as broad. Lokis generally gave people the impression of power; they were intimidating, both in height and breadth, but that's because they were bred for their superhuman strength.

But where Knight had a certain roguish appearance, owing to the shadow of stubble on his cheeks and jaw, Jax just looked scruffy—like he hadn't had a shower or a shave in who knew how long? His hair was longish on top and a deep chestnut color. It looked like a good haircut at some point in the past, but now it had grown out and no longer had style. The top section reached the tips of his ears, and the bottom was shorter, but uneven. A brown beard covered half his face. But neither his sloppy haircut nor his unkempt beard could mask the fact that Jax Rochefort was very handsome. And even worse, he carried himself in such a way that hinted that he was very aware it.

And that was just as well. If there was anything I couldn't tolerate in men, or women for that matter, it was narcissism.

"Why don't you two go out and take a break for a few?" I said to the two guards, Ernie and Judah, who had been with Knight when he came through the portal. Having taken their posts on either side of Jax's cell and refusing to utter a single word, they looked like beefeaters for the Queen. All they lacked were those tall, black, furry hats. Wally was sound asleep in his chair at the end of the hallway, snoring.

"Many apologies, but we have to man our posts," the one nearer me answered. I had a feeling he was probably Judah, only because the other guy had a country bumpkin sort of look to him and "Judah" didn't exactly strike me as a yokel sort of name.

I could hear the weres in their cells at the front of the hallway. They were talking amongst themselves, no doubt, wondering who their newest cell mate was. And the pixie was blatantly staring at us which didn't come as much of a surprise considering pixies are, by nature, damn nosy.

"It appears the lady would appreciate some alone time with me, boys," Jax announced with a sly smile. He stood up from his cot and lumbered over, wrapping his fingers around the prison rails. The shackles around his ankles had been removed, but remained around his wrists. When he was directly in front of me, I had to crank my neck to look up at him, he was so tall.

"Why is he still cuffed?" I asked the guard nearest me.

The guy shrugged as if the answer were obvious. "Can't trust him."

I wondered what there really was to trust when the guy was behind iron bars, but I didn't have to ask. Jax answered for me.

"Ah, yes, of course, no one can trust me as I'm a Loki and, therefore, the strongest they come." He laughed acidly and then wrapped his hands around the bar directly in front of him, pretending to pull it apart. "Perhaps I could even bust right through these cuffs and pull these bars apart before any of you can say 'oh, fuck.'"

I couldn't help my smile, but a millisecond later I forcefully banished it because I didn't want Jax to think I found him entertaining. When his attention moved from me to the guard, his smile dropped.

"Apparently I need to repeat myself. The lady said she wants some time with me alone, Barney Fife, so I'd appreciate it if you'd appease her."

"We got our orders," the guard to Jax's right said in a gruff tone, the one I guessed was Ernie. With his Southern twang and poor grammar, I thought the name "Ernie" suited him perfectly. Well, so would Barney Fife, for that matter.

"Now you're taking your orders from me," I announced, throwing my hands on my hips to let them know there was no room for argument. I had lots of questions for Jax and the sneaking suspicion he'd be more likely to give me the answers I sought if he didn't have a crowd.

"With all due respect, ma'am," Judah started, but I immediately shook my head.

"Don't 'ma'am' me! I'm the head of this branch of the ANC, meaning, I make the rules," I snapped, taking turns glaring at both of them. Out of the corner of my eye, I could see Wally waking up. He jerked a couple of times and rubbed his eyes before focusing on the guards and me for a few seconds. Then he hopped to his feet, but not before stifling a yawn.

Note to self, you need to write Wally up for falling asleep on the job, yet again, I told myself. *Freaking gnomes...*

"Dulce, you good?" Wally asked in a deep voice.

"I'm fine," I replied without bothering to look at him. Instead, my attention was fastened on Judah. I figured he was the guard in charge. But maybe that was just because he appeared to be more intelligent than Ernie. "I was just informing these two that I want some alone time with the prisoner."

"And I was informing her that we are under strict rules from Vander to stay where we are," Judah interjected, his attention never leaving my face.

"Not only am I in charge of this office," I started, narrowing my eyes at him, "but I'm also Vander's girlfriend." Truth be told, I didn't want to play that card, but I couldn't really see any other way around it. Jax made a whooping snort of a laugh and slapped his thigh with his mitt-like hand as he continued to chuckle. I ignored him, as did everyone else in the room. "So unless you want me to call him right now, and report that you aren't obeying a word I'm saying, I suggest you vacate the premises, and pronto!"

Judah paused for a couple of seconds before he glanced down at Wally, who had already made his way up to me. Standing beside me, all five feet of him, he said, "I'd listen to the lady," before nodding. "She's telling the truth; and she's got one hell of a temper!"

Judah paused another few seconds before he glanced at Ernie and then turned back to face me. "How long do you need?" he asked.

"Twenty minutes," I answered while continuing to stare him down. He just nodded as the two of them started up the hallway. A wave of relief washed over me.

"I'm feeling a piss and a coffee break comin' up for me," Wally announced, his way of exiting politely. He offered me a quick grin, which revealed yellow, uneven teeth. They actually resembled unpopped kernels of popcorn.

"Thanks, Wally," I said to his retreating back. When I returned my attention to Jax, I found him staring at me unabashedly.

"We finally find ourselves alone," he said, with another suggestive smile. I was more than sure that seductive expression had landed him more than a few bedmates. Well, that is, until he got locked up.

"You can cut the Casanova crap with me," I announced matter-of-factly. "There's zero chance that I'll let you out of here."

He threw his head back and chuckled heartily. "You do have a temper, don't you? Yosemite Sam wasn't lying."

Yosemite Sam was actually a pretty perfect nickname for Wally, considering how short he was, not to mention his flaming orange long hair and beard. But, regardless of the humor that image evoked, I wasn't interested in funny conversations. I had crucial information I had to squeeze out of Jax, and that was the only purpose for my visit. "I want to know why you turned yourself in to the ANC," I stated, studying him pointedly.

"Well, you certainly go straight for the jugular, don't you?" His eyes settled on my bust for a few seconds. I could tell it was a ploy; he was trying to make me uncomfortable.

"Answer the question."

"I already have." His eyes found mine again and he purposely yawned. "Go ask your boyfriend."

"Unfortunately, for both of us, he isn't here right now," I responded in a steely tone.

"Unfortunately?" he asked with a mock laugh. "Speak for yourself." Another suggestive smile appeared on his mouth. "I gotta admit, doll, I prefer it just the two of us." He studied me for a few seconds. "I believe in quality time."

"Enough of the sexual innuendo," I warned him, trying to keep my temper under control, because if he knew he could get to me, he'd just keep doing it.

"I apologize," he said with a pout. "I just can't help it when you're so damned sexy."

"Close your eyes then and try to pretend I'm a man."

Jax chuckled and shook his head. "Too late, madam, the truth has already been exposed." Then he sighed like it was a shame as he studied me for a few more seconds. "You're a fairy ..."

"Not important," I answered, and then figured I was just wasting my time. He wasn't going to give me any answers because he was too busy flirting with me. And I had no patience for someone who wasn't going to respect me. Spinning around on the ball of my foot, I started down the hallway.

"That's it?" Jax called out behind me. "That wasn't twenty minutes!"

"I'm not in the business of wasting my time," I responded over my shoulder, not bothering to slow down.

"I turned myself in because I wanted out!" he called after me. I stopped walking, but didn't turn around. Instead, I allowed him to continue talking. "I figured, with a new regime coming into power, now was as good a time as any to get out; so I turned myself in."

"And you pled for immunity in the bargain?" I asked, turning around to face him. I didn't take any steps closer though. I still wasn't sure if he were truly cooperating or not.

He nodded. "That I did."

"What about money? Relocation?" I asked, eyeing him narrowly. Of course, I could have gotten this information from Knight, but I wanted to hear it from Jax first. I planned to cross-reference his answers later.

"I didn't ask for anything, other than protection."

"What is the name of your operation?" I inquired, committing all of this information to memory. After our little interview, I'd be sure to write down everything he told me. That way, I couldn't forget any of it later.

"Crossbones," he answered stiffly.

I couldn't mask my surprise. Crossbones was the name of one of the larger underground potion operations in the Netherworld. They were probably right at the top of the list when it came to exporting the illegal stuff and distributing it on the Earthly plane.

"Turning yourself in was a pretty gutsy move," I played along, taking a few steps nearer him. "Apparently, you pissed a lot of people off."

"Of course, I did," he agreed with a nod. His smile seemed almost boyish due to the deep dimples on either side of his lips. "But you already knew that—it's the exact reason I'm standing here having this conversation with you."

"Because you wouldn't be safe in the Netherworld," I finished for him.

"If I were still in the Netherworld, I'd be dead by now."

I raised my brows, but didn't comment. Instead, I took the five or so steps that still separated us until we were soon facing each other, only the prison rails separating us. "So why did you want out?"

"Because crime doesn't pay?" he asked with a sidelong grin.

"Cute," I answered with obvious disdain. "But what's the real reason?"

"Can't a guy just ask for a change of scenery?"

"It's not that simple," I replied as I shook my head. "You're willing to risk death, or something even worse, by acting as an informant?"

"Isn't that pretty apparent by now?" he asked with a chortle. "But, damn, I have to admit: if I'd known how many hits I'd have out on me, I would have seriously reconsidered my decision."

"You still haven't told me exactly why you *made* the decision."

He shrugged. "You're obviously looking for an answer besides the one I'm giving you. But the one I'm giving you is the *truth*. I got tired of being a thug. And taking orders to kill people I didn't even know."

"You take orders?" I nearly interrupted him, finding this information interesting because I wasn't sure where he fell on the food chain.

"Everyone takes orders," he corrected me with another smug smile. That was ironic, considering he was the one standing behind bars and wearing chains.

"I was under the impression that you were at the top of the ladder?" I asked, fishing for information even though I wasn't under any impressions where Jax was concerned. Sometimes, though, it was better to play the part of uninformed.

"Everyone takes orders from someone," Jax repeated, this time, more slowly.

"So you had a boss?" Truthfully, I was disappointed. Why? Because that meant more work for us. Our main goal was always to get the biggest fish. Silly me for thinking he was exactly that.

"Yes," he answered, eyeing me with interest. "How long have you and Vander been together?"

"I'm the one asking questions here. You're not interrogating me," I snapped.

"Oh. Is this an interrogation?" he rebutted with practiced charm. "And here I thought we were just having a casual, albeit mundane, conversation."

"Who is your boss?"

"I'm afraid that information cannot be disclosed."

"Why?" I asked. "If you're truly on your way out, why continue to cover for someone else?"

"Because it was my choice. It had nothing to do with him. He treated me fairly. My decision is on me. So I won't rat him out."

"Okay," I said with a frown. "Then just tell me who runs your organization."

"That's simply a different way of asking me the same question," he pointed out as he shrugged. "Good try though."

"Then tell me who is in upper management."

"How long have you been with Vander?"

I inhaled deeply, trying not to let my annoyance with him get the better of me. "A few months," I lied. He didn't need to know anything about my relationship with Knight. As far as I was concerned, that subject was off limits.

"*I* was in upper management," he answered coolly.

"Okay, that's a good start. And where would you say you ranked in the pecking order?" I inquired, trying to understand exactly what role he played.

"Right below my boss," he answered with little interest. "I was one of the big guns."

"And who was your supplier?" I speared him with my narrowed gaze, trying to ascertain if he were being honest with me. "Or were the potions created in-house?" That was an interesting question. If their potion ring had purchased the contraband, he could possibly tell me what other rings were involved, if any. Well, if he was willing to part with that information, that is.

"You're asking me to divulge all my secrets," he said with a sly smile.

"Yes," I answered, frowning. "I thought that part was obvious?"

"But if I tell you everything, you'll have no reason to come back and visit me again," he explained with a shrug as he glanced around the small cell. "And I can't imagine what else there is to keep me occupied in here."

I sighed. "I know you don't know me, but the first thing you would know about me, if you did, is that I *detest* game-playing."

His smile broadened. "And I know you don't know me, but the first thing you would know about me, *if you did*, is that I believe life *is* a game."

I scowled at him while shaking my head as I tried to deal with the burgeoning anger inside me. "You do realize, don't you, that you can't have it both ways?"

"What do you mean?"

"You're asking us to protect you against the numerous threats you fear, but in return, you are required to give us information. It's not a one-way street."

He shrugged. "I've given you information already; and I intend to continue giving you information."

"But I have to play by your rules," I finished for him.

"You catch on quickly," he smiled, his flirtatious nature in full effect. "Any last questions before we retire for the day?"

I thought that was bizarre: him calling an end to our meeting when it was pretty obvious to both of us he had nothing else to do for the rest of the day. But I didn't argue. Instead, I took it as an opportunity to foist more questions on him. "Do you know who is responsible for the hits currently contracted against you?"

"I don't, but I imagine everyone involved does. You can't just retire from smuggling illegal potions without pissing off lots of people."

"I'm sure you're right."

"I usually am," he agreed, nodding, before his attention drifted to his fingers. He started to inspect his nails before facing me again, and his eyes suddenly began dancing. "Did you know I'm a Loki too?"

"I do."

"Do you wonder how I'd compare to your man?"

"No."

"Liar."

"I'm not lying," I said with a quick laugh of derision. It puzzled me why his candor didn't offend me like it should have. Yep, I'd definitely have to be careful with this one. His carefree, easy manner was undoubtedly masking a calculating, manipulative agenda. But, luckily for me, this was just another stroll in a very familiar park.

FOUR

That evening, I called Knight. I wanted to compare the information I'd pried from Jax with whatever Knight already knew about him.

"I can't talk long, Dulce," Knight said as soon as our *hellos* were out of the way. "I've got a meeting with Caressa in a few minutes."

"Okay, then I'll make it quick," I answered. No, I didn't appreciate how Knight basically had zero time for me lately, but the situation was what it was. Although I did understand it, that didn't mean I liked it. "I talked to Jax a bit today," I started.

"I prefer that you avoid him in the future," Knight interrupted me, his voice suddenly gruff. "He's not exactly someone I trust and what's more, I trust him even less where you're concerned."

"Well, he's also behind bars, bound by chains, and asking us for immunity. I think he's probably a little more helpless than you're giving him credit for."

"Don't be so quick to jump to conclusions," Knight argued. "Jax and helpless are two words that should never be mentioned in the same sentence."

"Well, *you* brought him to Headquarters! What did you really think would happen? That I would simply sit back and tell him to enjoy his stay?" My voice was growing increasingly irritated. As a rule, I didn't like him babying me, especially when I was a strong and very capable woman. Not only that, but I'd been working as an ANC Regulator for years, so it wasn't as though I'd never interrogated a prisoner before.

"I brought him to Splendor as a last-minute decision," Knight explained after a long sigh. "My main concern was getting him the hell out of the Netherworld. I didn't have time to predict what you would or wouldn't do with him." He took a deep breath. "But now I'm telling you in no ambiguous words: *I want you to keep your distance.* He's unpredictable, which makes him dangerous."

"Okay, point taken," I grumbled reluctantly. I didn't know enough about Jax to argue how dangerous he really was, or wasn't.

"Give me some time and I'll figure out what I want to do with him," Knight continued. "For now, however, just sit tight. He'll only be there for a few more days, at most."

Now it was my turn to sigh. Just when I actually felt like I could do my part to help with the new world order, my only opportunity was being ripped right out from underneath me. So now it would be back to the same old, same old. *Great. That's just great.*

"Well, I still have some information about Jax that you might find useful," I started, failing to mask the frustration and disappointment in my tone. "We might as well compare whatever we both learned about him so far."

"Okay, let's hear it," Knight answered. He sounded rushed, almost as if he were concentrating on more than just this phone call. In general, Knight, like most males, wasn't exactly the most competent multitasker. I always sensed when he wasn't paying attention.

"You start," I said while strange background sounds continued to waft over the line.

He cleared his throat and took a few seconds before answering. "For starters, Jax turned himself in a couple of days ago. That struck everyone as odd because he ranks fairly high in his organization," he said. I could hear the shuffling of papers on the other end and then his muted voice as he, no doubt, gave instructions to whoever was talking to him. Hmm, so it appeared Knight's multitasking had definitely improved. Yay for him.

"Jax told me he ranks only second to his boss whom he calls *the Kingpin*," I added. "So, I'd say he's pretty high up in Crossbones."

Knight was silent for a few seconds as more sounds of shuffling paper, mixed with muffled voices, persisted on the other end.

"Are you still there?" I asked, after another lengthy pause.

"Yeah," he answered immediately. "Sorry, Dulce. Anyway, yes, he's high up, but I'm not totally convinced he's as high up as he would like you to believe. Who knows for sure? Titles and ranks in these circles move faster than a starving vampire in a blood bank."

"Ha-ha, really cute," I answered, not able to keep the smirk from my tone even though I was trying to be a smart-ass. "So have you found out who his superior is?" I asked, putting on my detective hat again. "He wouldn't leak a syllable on that information, at least not for me."

"No, I can't say he's provided me with any info on that subject either."

I was more than sure my chances of getting Jax to open up were far better than Knight's. When it came to questioning men, women always seemed to have the upper hand. And Knight being the absolute alpha male that he was would only rub Jax the wrong way. Jax not only shared Knight's ancestry as a Loki, but also his competitive instinct and masculinity. And two alpha males in the same room could only result in butting heads and horn-locking.

"He's trying to reveal only a little bit of information at a time because he says he wants me to continue visiting him," I said with a frown.

"Of course he does," Knight replied, sounding more frustrated than I did. "He has eyes, doesn't he? Of course he sees how gorgeous you are."

"I'm not sure that's it," I said and sounded uncomfortable because I was uncomfortable. I definitely wasn't good at handling compliments.

"That's it for sure," Knight said, no amount of hesitation in his tone. "He's going to try to manipulate you into seeing him as much as possible." He was quiet for a second or so. "And I don't like the sound of that one bit."

"Well, if that means I can actually get something more out of him, isn't it worth it?"

"No," he responded immediately. "I would much prefer it if you would just leave Jax to me."

"I'm not going to do that," I said, figuring it was best to just come out with it. No use in beating around the bush.

I heard Knight sigh and I imagined he was wearing his angry face. "Dulcie, don't let him catch you off guard; and most of all, don't let him get under your skin."

"As if I'd let a potions smuggler get under my skin!"

"I'm just saying, be careful around him, Dulce," Knight repeated, his tone somewhat sterner. "My preference is for you to avoid him at all costs, and not imperil yourself at all. If I had it my way, he wouldn't be there in the first place. But, seeing as how he is, I'd really appreciate it if you left him the hell alone."

"Hmm, you almost sound like you're jealous," I announced with a laugh.

"Damn right I am!" he answered emphatically. "Why should that asshole get to spend his time with you while I'm stuck up here? Dealing with this clusterfuck?!"

"Ditto," I said, sighing deeply. "Ditt-freaking-o." Then, figuring the last thing I needed to do was focus on our crappy circumstances, I pulled my attention back to the main topic. "Can you at least cross-reference the stuff he's given us so far, and see if the stories match up?"

There was another lengthy pause and more shuffling papers. Knight then put the phone down on his desk to yell at someone, or so it sounded. He picked it back up a few seconds later, and continued. "We haven't gotten very much out of him yet," he admitted, sounding disappointed but still distracted. "Right now, unfortunately, I'm in the middle of extinguishing a series of more urgent fires."

"Isn't interrogating the second-in-command for one of the biggest potion-smuggling rings a big and urgent fire to put out?"

"Yes, Dulce, it is an important subject, no doubt, but Jax is not my priority at the moment," Knight breathed out, sounding irritated. "And, FYI, we still aren't sure if he really is the second-in-command."

"Point taken," I mumbled. "So?"

"So I still haven't figure out what to do with him," Knight admitted. "As soon as we knew about the death threats, I had to get him somewhere safe. Plan B is still being devised."

"Why don't you just leave Plan B to me?" I replied, even as I realized my chances of getting him to agree with me were probably nil.

"Dulce," he started, his tone of voice warning me not to argue with him.

But argue I would. "I can help you, Knight. It's not like I have a hell of a lot going on here anyway right now. Why don't you let me interrogate him?"

"Because it's a lot to take on," Knight answered immediately. "Jax knows what's up. He's been around the block and ..."

"And you don't think I'm capable of handling him," I interrupted, my lips tightening. I didn't realize I was holding my breath until my lungs forcefully exhaled it.

"I didn't say that."

"You didn't have to," I snapped. "I could tell from the inflection in your voice."

He sighed and grew quiet for a few seconds. "Dulce, you know you're great at your job, and I know you're great at your job; but you've never come across a Jax Rochefort before. He attained his stature for a good reason: he's treacherous and dangerous. It's not about my confidence in you, and it's not about me doubting your abilities. It's just that I don't want you anywhere near him! I don't even want him to know you exist! I don't trust him."

"He already knows I exist," I pointed out the obvious.

"Doesn't change the fact that I don't want you anywhere near him."

"You might not have a choice," I pointed out. "I mean, who knows how long you're going to be stuck out there? Meanwhile, he's here!" When he didn't respond right away, I continued. "Seriously, Knight, what's the worst that can happen? That I don't ask the right questions? Or he refuses to give me the answers we need? Maybe he'll feed me a line of bullshit? Regardless, those stakes aren't very high, Knight."

"That's fair enough," he replied with another distracted sigh.

"So rather than ignoring a possible gold mine, wouldn't it be better for you to coach me on how to interrogate him? Just tell me what information I need to get from him. You know your load is already too heavy, and dealing with Jax would be taking on more than you can handle right now." I inhaled a deep breath and figured my argument was persuading him because he wasn't arguing with me. Well, not yet anyway. "You know I can help you, Knight. Just tell me what I need to know about Jax, and advise me how to approach him."

"Dulce," he started.

"Help me help you," I finished.

"It's not that simple. You…"

"I know I can get him to talk," I interrupted. "It's not like I'm the new kid on the block. I've been doing this for a long time, Knight."

He paused for another few seconds. "You make arguing with you very difficult."

I smiled as soon as I heard his exasperated reply because it meant my victory. "You'd think by now, you could have learned that it's better to agree with me from the get-go; if only to spare us this back-and-forth."

Knight chuckled. "Guess I'm just slow." He was quiet for another few seconds and I heard the sounds of high heels clicking on the floor in the background. "And on that note, Dulce, I gotta run. Caressa just walked into my office. It looks like there's another emergency fire we have to put out. I'm sorry."

I could tell he was flustered. "It's okay," I replied calmly.

He'd given me the answer I wanted, even if I didn't have all the information I needed. Now I had the green light from Knight to discover whatever I could. Granted, I imagined there was no way he would find any time in the near future to come up with a prioritized list of questions for Jax, but I wasn't really concerned. I had faith enough in myself; I knew I could get the answers we needed from Jax. What was more, there was no way I was just going to sit on the treasure trove of information known as Jax Rochefort in the hopes that Knight would school me on everything he wanted or needed to know. Nope, I had to take the proverbial reins now and handle Jax all on my own.

And, really, whatever Knight didn't know couldn't hurt him.

"We meet again," Jax greeted me the next morning with a polished smile. Unbeknownst to him, his attractive smile was wasted on me. I'd already severed all relationships with my hormones and left them at the door. Now he was dealing with the cold, hard, fact-seeking Dulcie.

"I want answers," I said tight-lipped. I glanced at Judah and Ernie, but neither one said anything. They simply nodded their understanding before starting for the hallway, which was just as well because I wasn't in the mood for any arguments. I had no clue where Wally was, but I also couldn't say I cared.

I strode up to the prison bars and gripped them with my hands, leaning into Jax's cell as closely as I could. I wanted Jax to view me as his equal; and the only way to do that was by not showing any fear. I figured this was about as daring as I could get from a personal space standpoint.

"I was wondering when you might visit again," he answered in a charming tone. He took the few steps that separated us and stood in front of me, his cuffed hands wrapped around the bars beside mine. "It gets very lonely in here," he whispered, looking me up and down as obviously as he could. Even though he was definitely trying to make me feel uncomfortable, it didn't work. I was already fully prepared for it.

I stared at him directly and boldly. "I'm sure it does."

His eyes centered on my lips for a few seconds before he smiled, his gaze finding mine again. "If only you'd allow me a conjugal visit."

"We are both well aware that's never going to happen," I scoffed, trying not to sound offended. I'd already prepared myself for the possibility that Jax would escalate his efforts to get underneath my skin. It was entirely up to me to maintain an air of cool confidence and remain completely in control, even if I didn't feel it so much on the inside.

"Is it so far-fetched?" he asked with a shrug. "I have been told that I'm a very handsome man."

"You shouldn't believe everything you hear," I answered with an unforgiving shrug.

His smile broadened as he considered me with more interest. "And it probably goes without saying that I've had more than my fair share of eager women to warm my bed."

"I'm not here to debate whether or not you're attractive or discuss how many bed partners you've had," I replied, narrowing my eyes at him, "because I don't care."

"You don't care?" he asked, pretending to be taken aback.

"No, I don't."

"Then why are you here, Dulcie O'Neil?" he asked.

I felt my heart catch as soon as I realized he knew my full name. There was no doubt now that he was bent on trying to throw me off. This shocker was just another example of that.

"I'm here to offer you a deal," I continued without a hitch.

"Really? I'm listening."

"I expect you're sick to death of whatever crap they've been feeding you here," I started, studying him in a detached sort of way.

"I would eagerly agree with that statement."

"If you give me at least some of the answers I'm looking for, I'll spring for your lunch. You can order whatever you want."

He smiled, flashing his brilliantly white teeth. They contrasted nicely with his tanned skin and the brown stubble that was beginning to shadow his cheeks, jaw, and chin. Yes, he was decidedly attractive. No one could argue that point, not even me. Of course, it wasn't like I was really focused on Jax's looks though. I'd left my hormones at the door, remember?

"Whatever I want, huh?" he asked, eyeing me suggestively again. His gaze descended from my face, settling on my bust, before landing on the apex of my thighs, where he stared at me unabashedly. I held my stance and didn't flinch or wither. I'd prepared myself for this.

"Whatever you can *eat*," I amended.

He cocked his head to the side before his eyes returned to my face. "I have to admit, I'm quite partial to the taste of beautiful, young women," he started.

"And you can cut that crap out right now," I interrupted in an icy tone. "I'm not interested."

"If I didn't know better, I'd accuse you of being a lesbian." Then he cocked his head to the side and was quiet for a few seconds. "Although I have to admit, the idea of you with another woman might be exactly what I'm going to think about tonight, during my...alone time."

68

"Whatever I am is none of your business," I announced, choosing to ignore his latter comment.

"What if I intend to *make it* my business?"

"Then you're headed for a grand disappointment," I fired back. I felt the need to cross my arms over my chest as soon as his gaze returned to my breasts. But I resisted that urge and continued to stand there as if I were completely at ease, despite his scrutiny.

"Disappointed, huh?" he asked. Acting suddenly dejected, his shoulders slumped and he jutted out his lower lip. "And just when I was starting to get very excited about answering any, and maybe all, of your questions."

"I'm not on the bargaining table," I said as decisively as I could, "but lunch is. It's your choice to take it or leave it."

"What a shame," he responded while shaking his head and staring at me blankly for a few seconds. He seemed to be trying to determine if I was bluffing. I had to wonder if that was just another Loki trait—having the ability to see through anyone's poker face. If it were, it wouldn't have surprised me because it wasn't as though I had a catalog of each and every Loki ability. The longer I knew Knight, the more surprised I was at the extent of his talents.

"Call it whatever you will," I answered, "but my offer won't last forever; and I'm already growing very tired of playing your games."

"And to think how motivated I was to give you exactly the information you sought," he said, shaking his head like it was a big shame. All the while, though, he continued to stare at me as if he could see through me, to my soul. "It has been a while since I was with a woman; and you happen to be just my type."

"I should say I'm touched," I replied, shaking my head as a victorious smile became too hard to contain. "But I'm not."

"You're a tough one," he shrugged. Smiling as widely as I was, he continued, "But the question now is how much the information you're after is worth to you, and what you're willing to trade for it."

"I'm not willing to sell myself," I answered matter-of-factly. "As you can probably imagine, I'm not into breaking the law."

"You wouldn't be selling yourself, baby," he continued, his smile in full enticement mode. "We wouldn't be bartering for money."

His smarmy reply suggested exactly what we would be bartering. Even though his forwardness surprised me, I didn't let on. "Lunch or not?" I asked, taking a few steps back, my signal that I was tired of his games. "I'm a very busy woman."

"We both know that's not true," he argued with a hearty chuckle. "I've seen the goings on around here, which equate to zilch." He glanced to his left and his smile widened. "The only criminals you've got in here are those two wolves; and they've been here since before my arrival." Glancing to his right, at the suspended cage where the pixie lay sound asleep and snoring on her cot, he added, "Oh yeah, and the gnat in the cage."

"Lunch or not?" I repeated, trying not to sound flustered even though that's exactly what I was becoming.

"I'd say I'm the most exciting thing that's happened here in a very long time," he continued, grinning like a fool. "And I also could be the most exciting thing to happen to you, if you'd let me."

"Lunch or not?"

"You will eventually give in, you realize that?"

"No, I don't," I answered and shook my head. "And I'm about to tell Ginger, the cook here at Headquarters, to go ahead and count you in for today's lunch. My patience is fading fast."

"You love to play hardball with me, don't you?"

"I don't want to play anything with you," I responded, feeling the truth of my words all the way to my toes. "All I want from you are answers to my questions."

"I see," he said, that irritating smile of his still present and accounted for. "Well, would you like to know what I want from you?"

"No," I answered immediately. "All I want to know is whether or not I should order you lunch."

"You can order me lunch, but only if you eat yours with me."

I thought about it for a few seconds before I agreed, figuring this wasn't too much to ask. "Deal. What are we having?"

"I'm quite partial to Italian," he answered without pause. "An Italian submarine sandwich would hit the spot for me. Can't find a good one in the Netherworld, not for the life of me."

"Done," I answered as I whipped out my cell phone and called Mama Nona's. It was my favorite Italian delivery place and only a couple of miles away. I ordered Jax's sandwich and a plate of spaghetti and meatballs for myself before replacing my phone in my pocket. "Twenty minutes," I said with a smile.

"They're quick," he answered as his gaze landed on me again. "How do you stay so trim, eating pasta? You know it's crap, right? Wasted calories."

"And your sandwich isn't?"

He shrugged. "I'm a man and, hence, I don't have to watch what I eat."

"Charming," I replied with a heartfelt frown. "Let's see if you still feel the same way in a few years when your waistline has expanded so much, you can no longer see your toes."

"Guess, we will see, babe, but somehow I'm not too worried about that," he said as he smiled at me. "So does our social hour, er, our social twenty minutes, begin now, before the food gets here?"

"Is there any chance you're willing to talk business before the food comes?"

He shook his head. "That outlook is not favorable."

"Then I guess not," I answered with a sigh. My raised brow suggested I wasn't amused. Not that he let it sway him, because he didn't.

"So what would you like to talk about while we wait?" he asked, his contained excitement making him almost sound boyish.

"Are you scared?" I asked without thinking. I wasn't even sure why the question popped out of my mouth but it seemed to have a life of its own.

"Scared?" he asked, looking surprised that I would ask him this in the first place. "What do you mean? Scared of what?"

I shrugged, figuring my question wasn't that mystifying. "Are you scared that someone will come after you? Or are you scared about being found?"

"Of course I'm scared," he replied with emphasis. "Being scared all these years is what's kept me alive." He studied me for a few seconds before he opened his mouth again. "Anyone in my business who tells you otherwise is lying. Or they're already dead."

"Good answer," I nodded, slightly admiring his ability to admit as much. There was more to his compliance, however, than met the eye. I didn't believe he wanted to get out of the thug life, although I also didn't know what reasons motivated him to say he wanted to. That was one mystery I intended to solve.

"Next question."

"I'm sure you've seen what happens to rats who squeal, doesn't that make you nervous about doing what you did?" I tried to sound offhand, or like I was just making conversation. However, his answer to my question would tell me a lot.

He nodded, but didn't seem overly concerned. "I know what awaits me if I'm caught."

"And what awaits you?" I asked, sounding surprised.

"I've slit more than my fair share of 'Netherworldian neckties' over the years," he answered nonchalantly.

"Netherworldian neckties?" I repeated, knowing exactly what they were. In this case, though, I thought it better to act like an inexperienced ANC Regulator. Letting Jax think he could educate me was a good way to play him.

"Inform the ANC about any of our practices, and while you're still alive, your throat gets sliced open and your tongue is pulled out through it. You choke to death on the very same tongue that broke our trust," he described in a blasé tone and then nodded, even smiling at me in a sad sort of way, indicating he was well aware of the fate that awaited him.

"How poetic," I managed. "Better hope to hell we don't decide to give you back."

His eyes widened for a fraction of a second, then he apparently realized I was kidding. "Good one."

I shrugged and cocked my head to the side as if to say it wasn't so far-fetched. "All I can say is don't piss me off."

"You are the last person I would intentionally piss off," he said as his eyes began roving my body with no shame...again.

I frowned and sighed in obvious exasperation. "And just when I thought we'd moved on from that subject."

He laughed and held his hands up. "Hey, I warned you that it's been a while since I've had a woman. You can't blame a man for looking." His eyes settled on my bust again. "Are they real?"

"Of course they're real!" I responded before thinking better of it.

He just chuckled as he nodded. "They looked real although it is a bit hard to tell without feeling them. I've come across many a woman who swears her breasts are real but as soon as I touch them I can tell she's lying through her teeth."

"I can usually tell just by looking at them," I argued, frowning at him.

He eyed me narrowly, his smile almost contagious. "I'm feeling that lesbian overture from you again."

"You know I'm not a lesbian," I threw back at him. "I have a boyfriend, remember?"

"That means little to nothing."

"Really?" I asked with a laugh and a shake of my head.

"Sure. I think you're just confused. You think you want a man but really, you can't stop thinking about the softness of a woman, the way she smells, the way she feels."

"Don't confuse your daydreams with mine."

He shook his head as his eyes raked me from top to bottom again. "Nothing to confuse. You, my hot little captor, embody every one of my dreams, waking or not."

"You know, as a fairy, I could always magic myself into something you wouldn't find very attractive—like a troll, or a leviathan, or something equally as charming," I said. "Or you could behave yourself and make this easier on both of us. The choice is yours."

His smile dropped. "Well, when you put it that way ..."

"As long as we understand each other," I said with a wide grin, pleased to finally voice a threat that seemed to resonate with him.

"We do," he answered in a defeated tone.

"Good," I replied just as Elsie popped her head around the corner of the hallway.

"You ordered some food, Dulce?" she asked.

I stood up and started for the hallway. She met me halfway and handed me the brown bag, which smelled like heaven. Luckily for me, I had an active account at Mama Nona's. I paid them monthly for the privilege. Thanking Elsie, I turned to Jax, who continued ogling me lasciviously. Or maybe it was the food making his mouth water. I couldn't be sure.

Taking out his sandwich, which looked like an aluminum-foil wrapped torpedo and was roughly the same size, I attempted to pass it to him through the bars. He had a tough time accepting it, though, especially since his hands were still cuffed together. He glanced over at me with true concern in his eyes.

"It's next to impossible for me to eat with these things on," he said while holding up his wrists, as if I didn't know what he was talking about. "What do you think about springing me?"

I immediately frowned.

"It's not like I'll be able to do much harm since I'm still stuck in here," he finished as he nodded toward the bars that kept him hostage.

75

I studied him for a few seconds, silently debating whether or not to take his cuffs off. In the end, I figured he had a good point—he was still behind bars, so what difference could it make? Without another word, I held my hand out and made a fist. Then I shook my hand a few times until I felt a mound of dust in my palm. When I opened my hand, the ethereal particles glittered in the dim light. I threw them at Jax, bathing him in the opalescent specks and closed my eyes. I imagined his cuffs breaking apart and dropping onto the floor below him.

"Well done," he said.

I opened my eyes and saw the cuffs lying on the ground, directly in front of him. Then I held my hand out and made a sweeping motion toward myself. The cuffs responded by scuttling over the cement floor like some bizarre looking crab. Then they launched themselves between the prison bars and landed in a heap beside my feet.

"Don't say I never did anything nice for you," I said with a smile as he reached for the sandwich again and I handed it to him.

"Have you been to the Netherworld?" he asked while unwrapping the foil from around the sandwich. He wasted no time in proceeding to take a huge bite.

"Careful you don't swallow a finger," I reprimanded him, before thinking about the question he'd just asked me. Although I didn't want to give him any personal information, I knew that wouldn't get me very far. And, really, this question seemed innocent enough to answer. "Yes."

He nodded and swallowed an enormous mouthful before talking again. "Then you know what happens to fairies in the Netherworld?"

"Do you mean the wings bit, or the sexual crack bit?"

Upon undertaking the misfortune of traveling through the Netherworld, I'd immediately sprouted wings. They were more of a nuisance than anything else and randomly started flapping at the most inopportune moments. I had zero control over them. And the sexual crack part? In the Netherworld, fairies can make any male creature completely lose his mind in favor of his libido. I'd had a hell of a time keeping male creatures away from me, or getting anything with a phallus to take me seriously.

"The sexual crack bit," Jax answered with a deep chuckle that I immediately found charming against my better judgement.

"Yes, I'm well aware of that already," I muttered, "but thanks for reminding me."

"Luckily for you, we aren't in the Netherworld," he continued, shrugging in an offhand manner. "I doubt seriously whether I'd be able to control myself if we were."

"Lucky us then."

He nodded. "How long have you been working for the ANC?"

That was the question I kept hoping he'd ask me. My answer could either help significantly, or sadly hinder my relationship with him. "Not long," I said, hoping to hell he couldn't see the lie in my face. I assumed it was a safe lie since I'd never come across him before, even though I'd heard about his organization. Besides, I was such a small fish, no one in the Netherworld would have any reason to know about me. Well, no one who mattered anyway. "I was just hired on pretty recently actually."

"So you're a newbie and, hence, no one trusts you with a prison full of inmates so they sent you here?" he asked, motioning at all the empty cells surrounding us. He took another huge bite and polished off the remainder of his sandwich. I viewed my pasta and noticed I still had a long way to go.

"Right, this place doesn't exactly have a lot going on. Hence why Knight brought you here. He figured this prison would be under any and everyone's radar."

"If you weren't so nice to look at, I might actually be offended that I've been left in the care of a new cadet," he continued.

I shook my head. "That's not entirely true. You do have Judah and Ernie."

He frowned. "Right, and what exactly would they be able to protect me from?"

I shrugged to say I didn't have an answer for him. "Well, luckily for you, this is a small town and easy to overlook. So if anyone is searching for you, this would probably be the last place they'd look."

"It's just a matter of time before someone locates me," he said with a shrug. Then, his eyes settled on me and narrowed. "And who's to say what they'll do to you? Although we both have a pretty good idea, I'd wager."

"Let anyone try," I answered with steely resolve.

He didn't reply but just nodded before his eyes dropped to the plate of spaghetti in my lap. "You gonna eat all that?" he asked with sincere interest.

FIVE

After we finished eating our lunch, I managed to breathe a little more easily because it meant the time for idle chitchat was over. I was increasingly anxious to move on to the more serious questions that needed answers. Well, that is, as long as Jax decided to play by the rules he'd previously agreed to ...

"Okay," I started, watching him polish off the last bite of my spaghetti and meatballs. He'd already downed his submarine sandwich, which, in a word, was ... large. The dude had a serious appetite. 'Course, being the size of a Titan, what did I really expect? "I have questions and you have the answers."

He smiled immediately but it was a smile which unsettled me. Why? Because it reminded me of the Cheshire Cat—something mildly perverse. At the same time, his grin also hinted that he still had the upper hand, or believed he did.

"You certainly are a woman who cuts right to the chase."

"I wouldn't say that," I replied as I shook my head and regarded him coolly. "Case in point—we've been sitting here for the better part of thirty minutes, talking about a whole lot of nothing."

"Ah, yes. And for that, I am very grateful, and will forever be in your debt," he said in a mocking tone to which I didn't respond.

He sat back on his cot and plopped both of his large feet out in front of him, stretching his arms above his head before exhaling audibly. Even through his prison uniform, I could detect his bulky and sculpted arms, as well as his defined chest. This guy was strong, probably as strong as they came. It was something I didn't dare lose sight of. If the shit hit the fan and I ever found myself squaring off against him, I had no idea what would happen. Actually, that wasn't true ... I did know what would happen. My fairy powers would be useless against a Loki; meaning, I would basically be as good as dead. Well, that is, unless I had my Op 6 loaded with dragon blood bullets. Then *he'd* be as good as dead.

"Funny, Jax," I answered with a straight face. Clearing my throat, I let my poker face take over as I remembered the mountain of information I still needed from him. I wasn't sure how willing he would be to part with any of it. "So, you were the second highest in command in Crossbones?"

"You have a good memory," he answered in a slightly patronizing way, which started to irritate me. Then I reminded myself that I shouldn't take anything Jax said, or did, personally.

"How many people are below you?" I asked.

He shrugged and clasped his hands together above his lap. He looked about as contented as was possible, given that he was jailed and lying on a hard cot which, by definition, wasn't exactly comfortable. "Ah, maybe three hundred or so foot soldiers obey my command."

I didn't know what to make of that number at first—whether that was a lot of people beneath him or not a lot. But the more I thought about it, the more it concerned me, because Crossbones was only one in a bunch of potions rings. And if each of the crime rings operated with a few hundred or more members, that was definitely bad news for the ANC.

"How does Crossbones compare to other potions rings in the Netherworld, in terms of troop numbers?" I asked. I immediately remembered Knight saying something about the various factions of potions organizations and how they were all vying for powerful positions in the new Netherworld order. That was a sticking point that bothered me. Knight also mentioned those rings relied on their strength in numbers, even if they couldn't cooperate long enough to pose any sort of serious threat to the ANC. Nonetheless, as far as I was concerned, any threat to the ANC had to be taken seriously. And I had a feeling it was simply a matter of time before the bad guys started to smarten up and assemble against the ANC, the bigger threat, in their minds.

"We're one of the bigger organizations," Jax answered with a shrug. "Mayhem might be tied up there with us by now, but all the others are smaller." Then he appeared to reform his answer. "'Course, seems they're growing bigger every day. Ever since your father got his ass killed, we've been eager to see one of our own take his place."

"How did you know Melchior was my father?" I demanded while eyeing him narrowly. My stomach dropped to my toes as my breath caught in my throat. He'd acted so nonchalant about throwing that point out there; and yet, I was more than sure he knew exactly what he was doing. Yes, Jax was definitely good about keeping me on my toes. I had to be just as good at keeping him on his.

"You know, this cot is mighty comfortable," he said with a knowing smile. Then he tapped the open space of cot beside him. "I could move over and make enough room for you to squeeze in that tight little ass of yours?"

"How did you know Melchior was my father?" I repeated. My voice sounded like shards of glass scraping over metal.

"Or if you're still a little shy, I could just scoot all the way over and we could sit side-by-side until you warm up to me?" He smiled lasciviously as his attention fell to my hips. "Either way, I'm dying to get up close and personal with that fine ass."

"Cut the crap," I warned him, my heart racing. "How *did* you know Melchior was my father?"

He shook his head, like that information was no big deal. "I'm in the business to know, baby. It's *what I do*."

"Who told you?" I persisted, trying desperately to regain control of myself and the situation, but there was no denying how shocked I was by his zinger.

"No one who matters."

So he wasn't going to confess anything, meaning, I'd have to let it go. It seemed the harder I fought, the more Jax dug in his heels. Granted, it was beyond frustrating, but I chose not to focus on it. I had to move on. After pondering his admission that the crime rings intended to see their own gain power in the Netherworld, instead of Caressa, I decided that juicy tidbit was something I should further explore.

"So do you think any of these gangs are a real threat to the ANC?" I asked, putting to rest the question of what else Jax knew about me personally. I sensed he had more ammunition with which he'd zing me again, when the time was right.

Jax was silent as he appeared to consider my question. He theatrically drummed his long fingers against his thighs and then whistled absentmindedly for a few seconds.

"Really?" I asked, shaking my head with obvious irritation. "Do you have any idea how completely annoying you are?"

Glancing over at me, he smiled broadly, his dimples in full effect. "I admit that I actually enjoy annoying you. It's just so easy."

"That's probably true," I agreed with a heartfelt sigh. "But I also have to hand it to you: you appear to be irritating by nature."

"Ouch," he said with a chuckle that rocked the entire cot. Then he stopped laughing and inhaled deeply. "I think you're probably right—I seem to have the innate ability to get under anyone's skin." His gaze dropped to my bust, before landing on the junction of my thighs. "And I'm not sure about your skin, but I'd love to get inside your panties."

"Your charm knows no bounds," I answered with a faux smile before taking a deep breath and changing the subject. "So, let's get back to the potions rings," I began again, giving him an expression of impatience and pronounced discouragement. "Do you think they pose a real threat?"

"Yes ... and no."

I waited a few seconds for him to explain, but he just sat there, smiling at me dumbly. "*Yes and no?* What does that mean?" I hated having to force the subject, and was unable to hide my irritation. I knew I should have kept a better handle on myself, as well as my reactions to his annoying comments, but Jax was beginning to exasperate me. And if there was one thing I knew about myself, it was that I lacked patience.

"Yes, from a pure numbers standpoint; the rings have power. No, because they'd have to band together to have any hope of defeating the ANC; and I don't see that happening anytime soon."

"Why not?"

"Why not what?" he fired back at me. "Why would I love to get into your panties? Well, for starters, your body seems to have been designed for pleasuring a man and I'm a definite boob man. Although that ass of yours is starting to make me rethink my stance ..."

"Oh my God, will you give it a rest?" I demanded as I exhaled my frustration, even as I warned myself to calm down.

"I'm hoping I'm breaking down your resistance."

"All you're doing is giving me a major headache," I admitted, none-too-happily. "So unless you want me to leave right now, stick to your end of the bargain and answer my questions."

"While I will admit that if you did decide to leave, I would enjoy getting an eyeful of that round little ass of yours, I promise I'll be good from here on out." Then he stopped talking to smile at me. "Deal?"

"As long as you're being sincere."

"I am."

"Okay, deal," I answered, still giving him a frown so as not to encourage him. Then I cleared my throat and returned to the subject at hand. "Why don't you see the potions rings banding together anytime soon?"

"To make a long story short, we hate each other almost as much as we hate you Regulators," he replied with another laugh.

"So let's say you put aside your differences temporarily with one another?"

He nodded. "It would take a strong liaison between the top three rings; or maybe the top ring and four to five smaller ones," he concluded before taking a deep breath. "The ANC is still too powerful a force for any one ring to take on and expect to win."

"So if you joined forces with two or three rings, do you think you'd be powerful enough to go against the ANC and ultimately prevail?"

"Yes," he nodded. "Something like that." Then his smile broadened. "But don't worry your pretty little inexperienced head about it. Leave all the problem solving to the problem-solvers."

Angry heat filled my cheeks, but after a few deep breaths, I managed to maintain my composure. He was trying to get under my skin again, to throw me off. It was my sole responsibility to prevent him from succeeding. The truth was that Jax knew exactly which buttons he needed to push with me. And he'd figured it out in record time …

What was becoming more and more evident was that even though Jax was our prisoner, we were by no means in the driver's seat. He still had us where he wanted us; and it was up to him whether or not he released the information we were after. Yes, we could have always tossed him out onto the streets and left him to fend for himself despite all the death threats he was convinced were out there. But the chances of us abandoning him were nonexistent.

If he refused to give us what we sought, the worst that would happen was he'd remain our prisoner. I had a feeling he was okay with that. On the other hand, if he answered all of our questions, and we could prove the truth in his statements, of course, we would provide him with the protection he desired. At the very worst, he'd only become another inmate in a system where protection was somewhat standard. So, in reality, there was nothing left for me to threaten him with, which left me in a very precarious position.

"What other organizations could you unite with?" I asked, pretending like I hadn't heard his last comment.

"Not me," he corrected. "I'm out now, remember?"

"What other organizations could Crossbones unite with?" I rephrased, albeit glumly.

He shrugged as if to say he didn't know. "I didn't say Crossbones was looking to join up with anyone."

I frowned to let him know I wasn't swallowing his BS. "There was no reason for you to bring up that whole *uniting against the common enemy* bit if your organization never even considered it!" I exclaimed. "And I'm sure your boss is more than intent on seeing himself as the new Head of the Netherworld."

"Of course," Jax answered quickly, drawing his eyebrows together in an expression of mild irritation. "But who wouldn't?"

I, for one, wouldn't. But I didn't admit that much to him because I didn't want our conversation becoming personal again. I was having a hard enough time trying to steer it away from me and my "tight little ass" as it was.

"So, tell me, Jax, based on your evaluation of the nature of crime rings, and their requirement for strength in numbers, doesn't it follow that Crossbones would try to team up with other rings, if only so your boss could take the place of Melchior?"

"There is more than one way to skin a cat," Jax replied loftily.

"If we call that way number one, then what's way number two?" I asked, but Jax immediately shook his head, obviously refusing to answer my question. Rather than growing impatient or angry with him, I swiftly shifted to my next subject. "Tell me about the potions your organization supplies."

"What would you like to know about them?" he asked, his tone suddenly more childish and fun. "What colors they are? What do they taste like? Which one is my favorite?"

I inhaled deeply while reminding myself to stay cool despite how far beyond tiring he was becoming. "I'm starting to reach the conclusion that you are incapable of answering any question without trying to drive me to insanity."

"Maybe I simply want to see what you're really like when you drop that reserve of yours you're trying so hard to maintain," he answered. Sitting up straight, he then leaned forward, his eyes never leaving mine. "I'd love to know what Dulcie O'Neil is like when she's spontaneous, and not pre-calculating every word."

"Who says I do that?"

"I can read you like a book," he answered with a shrug. "You're trying so hard to play the tough cop; but inside, you're nothing more than a little, scared recruit. An amateur who is trying her best to fill shoes that are two sizes too big."

Great! He'd bought my lie about being new to the ANC. That was good. The less he knew about me, the better. That he knew Melchior was my father still unsettled me, but maybe he'd just surmised as much from our last names. And if such were the case, I'd already given too much away by admitting it. *Damn.* Score for him.

"I'm not scared," I responded in a matter-of-fact tone. He stood up and approached me, gripping the bars in front of him. I didn't flinch or take a step back; I held my ground, bent on proving, once and for all, that I wasn't afraid.

"I wonder how scared you'd be if you were locked inside this cell with me right now," he started in a low voice.

"I would never put myself in that position."

"Would I beat you senseless?" he continued, as if I hadn't said anything at all. "Or would I push you against the wall, wrap my hand around your throat to keep you immobilized as I found out for myself what that tight little ass of yours feels like?"

I swallowed hard. No, I gulped audibly. I couldn't help it.

Dulcie, keep yourself together! He's just pushing your buttons. You can't react! I told myself, trying to ignore the fires of indignation inside me that raged. My hands were already fisted at my sides of their own accord. It took all my effort to talk myself down from the precipice. My temper flaring, I was ready to go, and full steam ahead. But once that happened, I knew I wouldn't be able to rein it back in. So it couldn't happen.

It took me a few seconds before I found my voice again. "What sort of potions does Crossbones supply?"

He eyed me narrowly for a few seconds, apparently disappointed I hadn't lost my cool. Then a smile formed on his mouth as he pushed away from the bars. He walked to the far end of his cell before turning around and walking back toward me. He reminded me of a tiger trapped in a cage far too small.

"We've got the standards: ArsonFire, Marsh Root, Angel Breath," he began with a shrug before pacing back to the other end of his cell again. "But you can pretty much find those anywhere."

"But those aren't all Crossbones supplies?"

"You'd be right on that supposition," he affirmed while approaching me again. "There are only two potions we are known to exclusively provide," he continued, this time pausing right in front of me. "Thissel and DragonFire."

Thissel was a relatively new street potion. I'd only come across it three or four times in the last few months. A small, black pill, the size of a Tic-Tac, it looked innocuous enough, but when placed beneath the tongue, it instantly dissolved, hitting the blood stream relatively quickly. Thissel was also addictive in its sense of euphoria, which could last as long as a few days. The worst side effect to the euphoria, though, was the victim's inability to keep breathing. Take too much Thissel, and you could end up with permanent brain damage, or comatose.

"I haven't heard of DragonFire," I admitted, being careful not drop my guard or allow myself to appear uncomfortable despite his rigorous, penetrating stare. Truly, his incessant wolfish glances were nowhere near as off-putting as all the crap that came out of his mouth.

"That's because it hasn't hit the streets here yet," Jax explained with a quick shrug of his immense shoulders. Pushing against the cell bars, he extended his arms out straight in a stretch. He again reminded me of a large, feral cat in captivity. Definitely an apex predator. "We were working on widespread distribution."

"What is DragonFire?"

"It's much more addictive than Thissel," he said while crossing his large arms over his immense chest. If things were different and I hadn't been spoken for, or I wasn't a Regulator, and if he'd never started with his insulting comments, I might have actually considered him attractive.

"Great," I said, suggesting the polar opposite.

"In fact," he continued, sounding pedantic, "it's the most addictive substance available. In every clinical test case we've performed, once it's taken, the user is hopelessly addicted."

"You're kidding me, right? You actually test your narcotics?"

"Of course—that's the only way to know which ones are the most potent; and, therefore, which ones to market." He paused for a second or two, stifling a few more yawns, before returning his attention to me. "And thus far, DragonFire has exceeded everyone's expectations, owing to its addictive results upon first ingestion."

"That's gotta be good for distribution and, more specifically, for your bank account," I replied sarcastically.

"DragonFire could revolutionize the whole industry of street potions as we now know them," he agreed, apparently missing the irony in my voice. "Think about the potential numbers involved when anyone who takes DragonFire is immediately addicted."

"I already have," I continued dryly. "The possibilities are endless."

"Exactly," Jax concurred.

"So what are its effects? What's the draw?"

"Nothing," he replied with a shrug and a smile. "It does absolutely nothing!"

"It does *nothing*?" I repeated, frowning as I shook my head because I wasn't following him. "What do you mean, *it does nothing*?"

"There's no reason for it to do anything other than get the user addicted to it," he explained, taking a seat on the cot again and leaning back against the wall. "If someone tries it once and gets addicted, there's no need to infuse it with anything else."

"That makes no sense," I countered.

"No?" he asked. "Think about it. What is the main goal of all of these rings? What are they really trying to sell? Chemical dependency, of course."

"Right, but usually that dependency arises from a unique high, which the potion promises to provide. The reason anyone takes a potion is to achieve an otherworldliness; a blissful feeling that only the potion can provide."

"Right! And the reason someone would try DragonFire is no different."

I frowned and shook my head. "You just told me it doesn't give you a high or anything else, for that matter."

"Exactly! It doesn't!" he repeated with a large, smirky smile that made me more irritated.

"Okay, so, logically speaking, why would any sane person want to try the stuff if the only thing they can expect is becoming addicted to it?" I asked, voicing the obvious.

"Because most of them won't know that it doesn't supply any sort of high until it's too late. Once they try it, they're ours for life! The damage is already done. It's an instant money-maker!"

"But how do you market something that doesn't provide any stimulation in the first place?" I persisted. I totally failed to see how such a drug could gain any popularity at all. Once one person was victimized, he or she could warn the others. It seemed like the most important drawback was being overlooked, case studies or not.

"What motivates most people?" he asked, and I shook my head. I wasn't sure where he was headed. "Hope, of course. And hope, my dear, sexy ANC Regulator, is what compels them to get caught in our net."

"So your plan is to cash in on the chances that people will try DragonFire merely because of the hope that they will like it?" I asked. I wanted to make sure I understood his point. "That seems like a lot of ifs to be betting on, don't you agree?"

"Well, personally speaking, I have no intention of cashing in on anything. I'm out of the game, remember?" I didn't respond, so he continued. "But, yes, that's the idea; and no, it's not completely illogical at all. The contrary actually. "

"How do you figure?" I asked, frowning. "What's stopping a potential user from asking someone who already knows about DragonFire whether or not it's worth it? Most people get turned on to something by word of mouth. And word of mouth can't help you in that case."

"Exactly the opposite, my dear."

"How so?" I demanded, throwing my hands on my hips in frustration.

"Because as soon as someone tries DragonFire, what does that mean?"

"Instant addiction," I answered, hating to be quizzed. But Jax was difficult in general, so it came as no surprise. I hated to admit it, but I had a feeling all of his eccentricities were starting to grow on me.

"Right, and if one person is addicted to something, what does that advertise to someone else?" he inquired. His arcane attitude made me want to slap the smirk right off his face.

I took a deep breath and reminded myself that our conversation was essential for the bigger good. "That their addiction must be well worth it," I said softly as his points started to sink in. Only now did I realize how ingenious and insidiously dangerous this new street potion was.

"Exactly," Jax said with another swashbuckling smile. "So what do you deduce might be the biggest benefit for Crossbones?"

"That you don't have to experiment with more ways to alter someone's consciousness," I answered. "You only have to bother doing the first step of the process, not the second."

"And she hits the ball right outta the park!" he announced, smiling, despite my frown. "Our sole focus and emphasis on creating DragonFire was the addictive factor. By not spending further time or effort in creating a new high, we instantly saw a huge savings in time and money. The effect, or the high, of the potion is always the sticking point—it's the part that takes the most amount of time: testing potions, mixing them, finding the strongest ones, and the list goes on. Without that complication, the time it takes from production to market speeds up considerably, and with minimal investment."

"And what exactly is the minimal investment then?"

"If you're asking what it is financially, I don't have an exact figure. But what I can say is that all the proceeds and money are reinvested into assuring the potency and addictiveness of the potion. And our financial responsibility ends there. Once we have the recipe down, it's just a matter of mass production and distribution."

"So you do manufacture it yourself?" I asked, jumping on the fact that he'd just answered my next question without even realizing it. Or maybe he had, but didn't care.

"Yes, we manufacture all of our potions.

"How?"

He shrugged. "We have numerous witches on staff—all highly competent in their craft."

"And they were the ones responsible for divining the DragonFire recipe until it was as addictive as possible?" I asked, now genuinely curious as to how it all worked. Up until now, I'd only experienced the distribution side of the street potions scene—busting those who sold or used potions on the streets of Splendor. Lacking a lot of experience with the

Netherworld in general, I wasn't familiar with the behind the scenes aspect. This was definitely a learning experience, and then some. Well, that is, if everything Jax was telling me was true. Strangely enough, I did believe him.

He nodded. "We also have some sorcerers and warlocks on staff."

"Interesting," I said, mentally filing all the information in my head. I couldn't wait to inform Knight about everything I'd just learned. But first, I had to finish up with Jax.

"Is it?" he asked, smirking at me. "Do you find me interesting, Ms. O'Neil?"

"You know I do," I answered without pause. "Your life is very different to mine; but one I need to understand in order to become a better Regulator. So, of course I'm interested in you." I decided to play the *new cadet* card again, hoping it would somehow help me later. Why? I wasn't sure; but I went with my gut feeling anyway.

"I find you very interesting, myself."

"I know, but not for the same reasons that I find you interesting."

He shrugged before exhaling audibly. "I admit your ANC position is less than thrilling in my eyes, but everything else about you piques my curiosity."

"I would venture to say the only thing about me that piques your curiosity is what's inside my pants."

"That isn't true," he argued with a frown. "I find your personality ever so intriguing."

I laughed and shook my head. "Is that what you tell all the girls?"

"Just the ones I'm serious about... serious about bedding."

I shook my head again and exhaled audibly as I tried not to let his comments ruffle my feathers. Instead,

I tried to play the part of curious. "Do lines like those ever really work because I can't imagine they would."

"Lines?" he repeated, appearing puzzled.

"Don't play dumb with me," I said with another acidic laugh. I was now well beyond tired of him. "You can't actually think that I believe any of the crap that just came out of your mouth?"

Jax was spared the need to respond when the ground beneath us started to rumble and sway as if we were in the midst of an earthquake. But this felt very different from a quake, although I couldn't put my finger on why it was so different. A loud burst reverberated through the air. Moments later, it faded away to silence, as if it had never been.

My heart climbed into my throat as I caught my breath. My wide eyes met Jax's, but he didn't look surprised at all. On the contrary, his expression revealed a complete lack of concern.

SIX

"What the hell was that?" I asked Jax as soon as the rumbling died down. My heart was tightly lodged in my throat, but still pounding like an SOB. I was panting so hard, I was finding it hard to breathe.

"An earthquake?" he asked, but his lack of surprise or concern threw me. Furthermore, I didn't see any fear or anxiety in his eyes, which I found odd.

"I don't think so," I said, studying him pointedly.

But he simply shrugged as if he didn't have an answer for me and wasn't concerned enough to try to find one. His reaction initially struck me as strange, but I was too nervous to focus on it, or him. Instead, I glanced to my left and then to my right in an attempt to take stock of the room. Nothing seemed to be damaged as far as I could tell.

As soon as I looked back at Jax, the floor beneath me started to heave back and forth, then up and down. This time, I was a little more convinced that we could have been experiencing an earthquake, since the rumbling seemed faintly familiar. Wally's chair began to skip forward from the end of the hallway, and the pixie's cage swung back and forth violently, knocking her from one side to the other. I worried that it might pop itself right off the hook, which was coming out of the ceiling.

"Get me the hell outta here!" she screamed in her helium voice, as she clung to the bars of her tiny prison and beat her wings frantically.

Meanwhile, the two weres in the holding cells located at the front of the hallway were also getting understandably freaked out.

"What the hell is that sound?" One of them yelled out, his tone revealing his panic.

"Earthquake!" the other one answered and due to my keen sense of smell, I could detect their increased perspiration. They both smelled earthier than usual.

"Let me out of this cage!" the pixie continued, but I couldn't say my mind was on either the pixie or the weres. Instead, I was trying to figure out just what the hell was going on because I still wasn't convinced we'd just experienced an earthquake.

There was no sign of Wally, Ernie, or Judah, which was probably a good thing. Hopefully, they'd found cover, or were somewhere safer than here.

"It sounds like the rumbling stopped," I said as I faced Jax, who still looked completely unconcerned, bored even. Neither of us said anything else for the span of a few seconds as I stood stock still, testing the truth in my words. I looked down at the floor, studying it for a moment or two before I glanced back up at the walls, trying to detect if they were still moving. They didn't appear to be.

I returned my attention to Jax, who remained very solemn. No sooner did my eyes meet his than the floor started to shake again, making a horrible grinding noise as it did so. Jax immediately grasped onto the iron bars to remain upright. As the floor swayed beneath us, going up and then down again, my knees buckled before my legs flew out from underneath me. The floor suddenly shoved me forward and I was hurled headlong into the wall, landing beside Jax's cell. I had to brace myself for the impact with both arms against the wall to avoid breaking my neck or nose.

"Are you okay?" he called out, finally looking worried.

"I'm fine," I said as I tried to stand up but it suddenly felt like someone was pulling me backwards into the room with a pair of invisible hands. I started to trip over my own feet again and had to right myself against the wall, trying to stand in place long enough to plan my way back to Jax.

Regaining my balance, however, was nearly impossible when the ground continued to rumble and buckle beneath me like a feral horse. I fell over again, this time, landing on my butt. I was so freaked out, I couldn't register any pain and wasn't even sure if I was hurt or not.

Immediately rolling over, I got onto my hands and knees, assuming my chances for getting hurt decreased the closer to the ground I was. I inched forward, heading for Jax's cell. My only thought was to get us both to safety.

When I reached his cell, I tried to right myself again, but the floor kept swaying and rolling to such an extent, it made it impossible to stand up.

"Look to your right!" Jax yelled out as I glanced over my shoulder, only to see Wally's chair flying past me, one of its legs narrowly missing my head. It crashed into the wall at the far end of the room.

Dulcie, you have to take cover! I told myself.

The only problem was that there weren't any tables under which I could shelter myself, and the doorway to the hall was a long way off, which meant I wouldn't be able to secure myself inside the door frame.

"Just grab hold of the bars," Jax interjected, his voice much louder than the grumbling, angry quake.

"Nothing in the room can hurt you because it's all fastened down."

"You mean aside from that chair that nearly knocked me out?" I ground out while struggling beside the wall. The floor was rolling back and forth, but also jerking from side-to-side, and out from underneath me. It was impossible to walk, almost impossible even to stand up.

"Yes, aside from that," Jax answered. His smile seemed too nonchalant, given what was going on. "The only other thing to worry about are the lights in the ceiling; but those seem to be still intact. Grab the bars and hold on tight; you're about to have the ride of your life!"

Considering his was the only option I had, I leapt forward and wrapped my fingers around the bars in front of me. Just then the ground buckled beneath me and I felt myself drop. I tightened my grip around the bars and gradually lifted myself back up. Barely a half second later, the ground heaved upward again, and I worried my head would ram into the ceiling. My stomach climbed up into my throat and dropped again just as fast, making me feel sick. The vertigo reminded me of how it feels when you drive up and down a twisting, mountainous road at too high a speed.

"Woo hoo!" Jax yelled with a laugh that seemed way too excited, given the circumstances.

"What is wrong with you?" I screamed at him.

"The Gods must be pissed that I'm locked up!" he yelled back with an outstretched smile, his voice barely audible over the din in the room.

I couldn't respond because it felt like the floor was ready to give out beneath me. Gripping the bars of Jax's cell as tightly as I could, I hoisted myself upright again. I tried to catch my breath and tried even harder to stay standing, despite the ground breaking up and bucking beneath me.

"I got you now," he said. "Just don't let go," Jax said as he covered my hands with his and pushed his weight against them, obviously trying to keep me secured in place.

I didn't take a whole lot of relief from his comment though. If the seesawing activity of the ground got any worse, there was no way I could remain steady. And I doubted that Jax had a good enough grip on me to make him any more successful.

"Put your feet on the bars like I'm doing," he said. Glancing down, I noticed he was keeping the soles of his feet on the side of the bars. It looked like he was climbing on them like some sort of tree-dwelling animal. "You'll have to support the weight of your body with your arms," he explained.

"I don't know how long I'll be able to manage that," I admitted. My upper body strength was definitely inferior to my lower.

"You have no other choice," he answered calmly, narrowing his eyes on me in a serious expression. "The bars are the only things in the room that aren't moving."

On that point, it seemed he was correct. I checked out the floor again, and even though it didn't seem like the rumbling had gained any momentum, the ground continued to rise and fall beneath us as if we were on the sea, at the mercy of the waves. The incessant bobbing motion made it nearly impossible for my feet to gain any purchase on the bars, but I continued to try.

"This is no earthquake!" I shouted, shaking my head as I faced Jax again. He just looked at me vacantly, not bothering to respond. But, really, he didn't have to say anything because I was already convinced we were dealing with something else. As a native Californian, I'd had my share of earthquakes, and knew what to expect—usually a sudden jolt, followed by violent shaking that lasted for several long seconds.

But this shaking was very different. It was a rolling vibration that pulsed and throbbed through the ground beneath us. And it had been going on now for a few minutes, not seconds. It almost felt like something huge was beneath the floor, trying to escape, and causing the floor to arch up and drop back down again. Almost like a plow tilling the earth, but upside down.

"Dulcie! What's happening?"

Hearing Sam's panicked voice, I glanced over my shoulder only to find her staring at me, open-mouthed. She stood in the doorway of the jail cell and she wasn't grasping onto anything. She was also standing up straight, and it appeared as though the ground beneath her wasn't rumbling or shaking. But how was that possible when it felt like Jax and I were adrift on an angry ocean?

She took a couple of steps closer until I yelled at her. "Stay where you are!" I warned her. "Don't come any closer!"

As soon as the words left my mouth, my right foot slid off the bar. Then both of my feet landed on the floor again. As if reacting, the ground heaved upward and dropped down again, making me nearly knee myself in the chin before ramming my butt into the ground. Without even realizing what I was doing, I released the bars and plummeted to the floor.

"Get up and wrap your hands around the bars again!" Jax yelled at me. "You have to keep yourself off the floor!"

I nodded even though it was a Herculean effort to pick myself up and attempt to grip the bars again.

Once I was able to right myself, I lurched forward, narrowly missing the bars and landed, face first on the ground, which surged up to meet me. Luckily I braced myself with the palms of my hands so my face didn't crash into the cement.

"Get up!" Jax yelled.

I rolled onto my butt and then pushed myself up, all the while feeling like I was on a tiny boat in a rough ocean.

"Give me your hand!" Jax ordered as he released one of the bars and then stretched his arm through the opening between it and the bar next to it. I hoisted myself forward and gripped his hand as hard as I could, even as the floor completely dropped at least a foot or so underneath me.

But Jax's hold on my hand was sure and strong and with one healthy tug, he pulled me right up to him.

"Grab the bars!" he said as I wrapped my hands around them, straining to stay upright, and trying desperately to control my flailing legs. I made several attempts to get my feet up and onto the sides of the bars, but my arms by then were physically exhausted.

"I can't hold on," I said, sounding defeated. "My arms are too tired."

"I will help you," he answered with a quick nod as his eyes bored into mine. "Your only job is not to let go."

"I can try," I said but there was no way I could continue holding on like he'd instructed me. Instead, I wrapped my legs around the bars as tightly as possible. Jax also helped ensure I wouldn't fall off the bars by tightening his grip on my hands until his knuckles turned white.

"Dulcie, hold on!" Sam yelled out and when I turned to face her, I noticed she'd taken a few steps back up the hallway, apparently heeding my warning and avoiding getting into the thick of it, thank God.

"I heard something that sounded like an explosion! What's going on?" Elsie called out as she appeared beside Sam. She visibly held herself back from entering the room once she saw me hanging from the cell bars while the ground continued to buckle and roll beneath me. She wore the same expression of horror that decorated Sam's face.

"Something's beneath us! It's moving the ground up and down," I cried, figuring that was the only explanation that made any sense. And from what I could tell, whatever that something was, it was centered directly underneath Jax's cell, which meant Jax was directly in the line of fire.

I have to get him out, I thought to myself, even as I realized how futile my words were.

Futile because the only key to open the cell was located on a chain, which was currently wrapped around Wally's waist. And who the hell knew where Wally was? I would have attempted to open the cell with my magic, but the bars were reinforced with magical wards to make sure the only way to open them was with the key.

At the sound of the floor heaving beneath us, I glanced down, only to find it rippling and buckling, the concrete breaking apart as if it were as frail as pastry crust.

"Dulcie, get away from his cell!" Sam called back, her voice cracking. "Whatever is under the ground is directly beneath you both!"

"I can't leave him here by himself, Sam," I countered, audibly conveying my frustration. Not waiting for Sam's response, I addressed Elsie instead. "Elsie, get Wally! Tell him we need the key to the cell so we can get Jax out!" Elsie nodded at me before turning on her toes and running back up the hallway. I added, "And get back as quickly as you can!"

I prayed and hoped she'd find Wally immediately because I had no idea how much time we had before whatever lay beneath us would make itself known. And that was one moment I really didn't look forward to. Something that could burrow up through the ground and cause the floor to buckle and shake like it had only meant it was gargantuan in size ...

"Who knows how long it'll take Elsie to find Wally?" Sam asked. The sound of dread in her voice was more pronounced when she added, "It may take more time than you have!"

I refused to look at Sam because I wanted to avoid the concern I knew I'd see in her eyes. Of course, she wanted me to fend for myself rather than act the hero to a prisoner; but I didn't regard it the same way. Jax had come to us for protection; so it was up to me to provide it. The idea of turning tail and abandoning him to his doomed fate was something I would never consider doing.

"You know she's right?" Jax asked. "You should save yourself."

When I looked up, his gaze was already fixed on me. He didn't say anything more, but gave me a sly smile, acting like he wasn't as concerned with his predicament as I was. Well, good for him. Nice to know one of us wasn't taking the whole thing seriously. However, when he didn't loosen his hold on my hands, I sensed he wanted me there with him as much as my own sense of duty demanded.

"Why aren't you worried about what's going on?" I asked in exasperation.

He shrugged. "I can't control fate. My destiny is whatever it was intended to be."

"That's really poetic, but it's not much help," I grumbled with a frown and then shook my head to let him know I refused to accept his answer. Still, I had bigger fish to fry than Jax and his apathy in improving his own destiny.

Eyeing Sam, I tried to figure out how Jax and I could make it across the hallway. Well, that was, as long as I could get him the hell out of his jail cell.

I glanced down again and noticed the floor was actually starting to break apart, and pieces of concrete now stuck out of the ground at various angles. Not only that, but the ground continued to rumble, moving the jagged pieces of concrete every which way.

But our escape route wasn't my primary concern. The most important thing I could do right now was to get Jax out of his cell and then get as far away from it as we both could. But the whole *getting-Jax-out-of-his-cell* was the sticking point. There was still no sign of Elsie or Wally. And I couldn't, in good conscience, save myself while leaving Jax to fare alone. Being confined behind bars, he had nowhere to go and no way to save himself. He was basically a sitting duck, just waiting for whatever was underneath us to make itself known.

That was when something occurred to me. "Are they coming for you?" I asked as I wondered if someone from Crossbones was responsible for this...attack. Maybe someone had found out where Jax was and was now sending some enormous creature to eat him, or something even worse.

"I don't know," he answered as he shrugged. He still appeared very stoic, or maybe that was just his way of dealing with his own fear. "But you should stop thinking about me and start thinking about you," he finished as he released my hands.

"You know I won't do that," I replied. Shaking my head, I looked over at Sam, hoping to see Elsie and Wally beside her, but no such luck.

"Dulcie!" Sam yelled. "Please!" I couldn't look at her any longer because of the fear I could see in her eyes. I just shook my head and took a deep breath before facing Jax again.

"The situation isn't so bad that I'm going to give up on you," I said, having to yell the words because the rumbling inside the room was so loud.

As soon as my eyes met Jax's, the ground began to rock back and forth with renewed fervor. Once again, I could only cling to the bars of Jax's cell in order to stay upright. The sound of huge boulders grinding against each other grew unbearably louder. Pretty soon, it became as deafening as thunder.

"Oh my God!" I breathed out as I watched the floor at the far end of Jax's cell start to crumble away where it intersected with the walls. Pieces of the walls started to drop off into some sort of sinkhole.

"What the hell is going on?" I screamed as I gasped, watching more and more of the cement floor disappearing into the void and nothingness below. The blackness appeared to be consuming the ground, swallowing it, piece-by-piece. The brown soil of the earth and rocks appeared briefly beneath the floor before the earth simply collapsed into the deep tunnel.

"Dulcie, get out of there!" Sam yelled from the other side of the room with unbridled panic in her voice. "It looks like the floor is falling out!"

But I couldn't pull my eyes away from what was happening inside Jax's cell. I watched the small room descending into the ground, as if the darkness below were gorging itself on the floor. Chunk-by-chunk, the cement foundation fell into the black tunnel forming beneath us. I unwound my legs from the prison bars as I realized I had to make a choice—either get sucked down with Jax, or save myself.

There was still no sign of Elsie …

No sooner did my feet touch the ground when the floor shook uncontrollably in an up and down motion. As it rose up like a volcano, the floor inside Jax's cell caved into myriad pieces of concrete. The broken pieces dropped down into the huge abyss beneath us, the sound so loud I wished I could cover my ears. The gaping hole inside Jax's cell stretched beyond it, traveling all the way to where I clung to the bars.

"You need to get out of here!" Jax yelled at me.

Realizing he was right, I jumped down and turned around to get an idea of whether or not I could reach the area where Sam stood. After assessing the broken concrete slabs that blocked my path, I sincerely doubted I could climb over them. The entire floor was cracking and swaying apart. It shifted up and down like gigantic piano keys playing a quick symphony.

Another roar and the fault line that started between Jax's cell and the rest of the room suddenly widened into a valley that was at least three feet wide. It continued to expand as the floor shook, leaving Jax and me basically stranded on an island. We were totally surrounded by the growing chasm.

There was only one way out of our predicament, and I held the answer. Fisting my right hand, I closed my eyes. As my magical dust filled my palm, I opened my eyes and, glancing behind me, I threw the particles at the pieces of broken concrete, which reminded me of old tombstones being tossed from the ground.

My magic didn't go very far. All of the magical particles were immediately sucked down the chute of the black tunnel, disappearing from view before I ever got a chance to magick either of us out of this quandary.

"It's too late to try to escape," Jax called out, shaking his head. "If you try to reach your friend, you'll get swallowed up," he finished in a grave tone, apparently having witnessed my poor attempt to save us. "The only hope we have left now is to keep holding onto these prison bars. I'd take a lesson from them, because they aren't going anywhere."

When I looked at Sam again, there were tears in her eyes, which soon overflowed, rolling down her cheeks. "I'll be okay, Sam," I tried to reassure her, even though I didn't mean it. At this point, I seriously doubted whether or not Jax and I were going to make it out of this … alive.

Regardless, Jax had a good point. The bars seemed to be the only things we could hold onto while the floor inside the cell rapidly disintegrated. The iron bars weren't attached the floor, but to the walls, which, so far, seemed to be holding up pretty well. Wrapping my legs around the bars again, I now clung to them as if my life depended on it.

And it probably did.

"Oh, God," I whispered when the cot, which was bolted to the floor, started to shake. The floor beneath it began to break apart into chunks of concrete, each one vanishing into the blackness below. The cot, half of which was now hanging in the chasm, began to whine and moan as the suction of the tunnel tried to rip it out of the wall. The bed linens were stripped right off and sucked down the chute, the mattress immediately following. In seconds, all that was left were the metal slats and wire mesh that comprised the base of the cot.

"Dulcie, hold on!" Sam yelled. In the din of the wind tunnel, her voice sounded very small, and far away.

As the floor inside Jax's cell continued to fall into the void, the entire bottom of the cot was soon consumed. The upper half still whined while shifting this way and that. It was barely attached to the wall and appeared to be pulling itself free, taking with it the two enormous bolts that held it against the wall.

Meanwhile the floor continued to break apart, disappearing into the darkness below as if it had never been. In no time at all, more than one half of the floor in Jax's cell was gone.

The cot strained and scraped the wall before suddenly being yanked away from it as pieces of drywall and two-by-fours disappeared into the wide gorge, along with what was remaining of the cot.

I could feel the force of the vacuum generated by the black hole because my hair started to get sucked forward, between the iron bars.

"The suction is too strong!" I yelled out to Jax as the full force of the greedy wind yanked at my clothes. I had to shut my eyes tightly to keep them from watering in the fierce air current.

"Yes, it is," Jax responded, his voice devoid of any emotion. I opened my eyes immediately, just at the moment he let go of the prison bars. With his arms parallel to his body, he allowed himself to fall, dropping helplessly backwards, straight into the abyss.

"No!" I screamed, fear surging up inside me because this had to mean that Jax realized the futility of trying to resist the vacuum. And what did that mean for me?

"Dulcie, don't you dare give up!" Sam yelled at me, but I couldn't turn my face in her direction. The unending suction was suddenly positioned right beneath me. The pull of it was almost unbearable. I made the mistake of opening my eyes; and worse still, looked directly below me, where I couldn't see anything except the inkiness of the expanding hole.

I held onto the bars with all of my strength, keeping my eyes shut tightly against the incessant grasp of the air. As one of my legs suddenly unwound itself from the bars, I watched my tennis shoe get sucked right off my foot. It was quickly followed by my sock. Feeling an intense tugging on my pants, I heard the sound of the seams ripping apart. Seconds later, half of my pants were swallowed by the darkness below me.

You're not going to make it, Dulcie, I told myself, realization dawning on me.

NO! I screamed back at myself. *This can't be the way I go!*

But it looked like this was going to be the way I was going to die because there was no way in hell that I could save myself. The suction was like nothing I'd ever experienced. My other shoe and sock were suddenly ripped off as soon as my leg dropped from around the bars. It was just a matter of time before the other half of my pants would follow.

"Sam, I love you!" I screamed out as loudly as I could. Turning my head, I faced her, even though it took all my will power to do so. She stood there, crying so hard, she was unable to speak. All she could manage to do was shake her head before gallons of tears fell from her eyes. "Tell Knight I love him!" I added before the roar of the wind tunnel overcame me. I knew I didn't have enough strength left to fight it any longer.

I released my fingers one-by-one, before fully allowing the suction to envelop me in its darkness and condemn me to the tunnel and my fate.

SEVEN

With no idea what to expect, I released myself to the dark void beneath Jax's cell. At first, I thought I'd be killed as soon as the inky darkness enveloped me, but that wasn't what happened at all. My pounding heart proved I was very much alive. And I could feel the coldness of the air rushing past me, as well as the intense suction that relentlessly pulled me downward, taking me God only knew where.

I couldn't say if seconds or minutes ticked by as I fell through the darkness or maybe I was in a vacuum where time stood still. Either way, I couldn't see anything at all. I briefly wondered if I'd inadvertently closed my eyes because the rushing air made them water. But my eyes weren't closed, or I wouldn't have been able to see a faint light in the distance. It appeared to be coming from the bottom of the wind tunnel I was trapped inside. It was difficult to focus on the light, since I was still falling, and my body kept twisting and turning upside down.

When I found myself facing what I thought was downward, I noticed the light again. It started as a speck, but soon began to grow brighter and larger, the longer I stared at it. Several seconds later, I rotated around until I no longer could see the faint light, just the tunnel's darkness once again. I figured I had to have fallen pretty far down the wind tunnel, since I couldn't see Jax's cell at all anymore, not even the slightest flicker of light that might have hinted at its location.

I tried to swim back around again, hoping to face the tiny light. I assumed it was at the end of the tunnel, but trying to perceive it wasn't easy. Maybe it was due to how rapidly I was falling, or maybe it was the greedy suction that drew me through the tunnel, but for some reason, I couldn't seem to flip myself around.

As soon as I gave up on seeing the wavering glow again, it seemed like someone had turned on a light switch, because I was suddenly bathed in fluorescence. I immediately used my hands to shield my eyes from the harsh intensity of the blinding light. When that failed to relieve the stinging in my eyes, I slammed them closed. My eyelashes barely dusted my cheeks before I felt myself landing. I touched down on something that was too soft to be the ground and, yet, I still managed to land hard enough for the wind to get knocked right out of me. When I felt the pressure of hands on my back and under my legs, I realized I was in someone's arms.

"And that was a perfect catch on my part!"

I heard Jax's voice and blinked my eyes open while sucking in a few shallow breaths. I no longer had to shield my eyes because the light surrounding us was nowhere near as oppressive as it had been. Instead, it surrounded me in shades of light blue, almost like it was dawn or dusk.

"What happened?" I asked, feeling shell-shocked.

Jax shrugged like the answer should have been obvious. "A wormhole."

"A wormhole?" I repeated, frowning at him all the while. Although I'd never experienced a wormhole prior to this one, I vaguely knew what they were. They were similar to portals in that they would connect you from place A to place B. The only difference between the two being that wormholes were usually created with the express purpose of kidnapping someone ...

I glanced up at Jax's smiling face and then looked down again to see I was cradled in his large arms. And I was sans pants.

Yes, my missing pants concerned me, but not as much as the realization that I was here with Jax. Jax was a wanted man, both by the ANC and his own people which meant we could be in hostile territory, surrounded by both of our enemies. I immediately checked the area in front of me before doing the same behind me to ensure that I was aware of any possible threats.

"We're here alone, hot cheeks," Jax announced in a tone of voice that I found much too familiar for my liking.

But as far as I could tell, Jax was correct—it seemed there was no one else around, just us. And we appeared to be surrounded by numerous, and unusually tall ... pine trees? It was no surprise to me when I began panting. My heart was pounding so hard, I half wondered if I might suffer a heart attack. I had to take a few deep breaths before facing Jax again.

"Wh ... where are we?" I started before shaking my head as I wondered if I *had* just died, because this scenery didn't make any sense. I closed my eyes and opened them again, half hoping or expecting the environment to change, but it didn't.

"No can say," Jax responded with a shrug. I wasn't sure if he didn't know where we were or if he just wasn't interested in sharing. But I also didn't push the subject because I already knew I wouldn't get far.

"Great," I muttered as I took a deep breath and reminded myself that at least I was alive. Things could have been a hell of a lot worse. Only then did I remember he was still holding me and then I realized one of his hands was perched securely beneath my ass. "Put me down!"

"Okay," he replied before releasing me from the cradle of his arms. He took no precautions about placing me carefully onto my feet. Instead, he simply let go and I landed, butt first, on the ground below which was littered with pine needles.

"Ouch!" I yelled as I glared up at him and rubbed one of my offended cheeks.

"What? You ordered me to put you down!" he replied with a shrug while holding his hands up in mock surrender. "A simple thank you would have sufficed."

"For what?" I snapped. "I should thank you for dropping me right on my ass?" I stood up to brush the impaled needles from my butt.

"No! Thank me for catching you when you plummeted out of the wormhole!" Jax answered. "That was practically a superhuman accomplishment!"

"Well, as a Loki, you're not exactly human to begin with, are you?" I grumbled. After inspecting my sore butt one more time, I also remembered I was nearly naked from the waist down, except for my panties. And Hallelujah for those. Jax was more than enjoying my predicament by narrowing his eyes on my ass, and then my crotch, until I slammed one hand in front of my thighs and used the other to cover my cheeks. He just laughed at me.

"No, I'm not a human," he replied before taking several calculated steps to the side so he could more easily observe my backside. I muttered something under my breath that was so unintelligible, even I couldn't understand it. Then I moved to the side to prohibit him from further glimpses of my family assets.

"I have to admit, I was very pleasantly surprised to find myself up close and personal with that great ass of yours," he jibed with a shrug. He continued to skirt around me as I continued to thwart all his attempts to improve his view.

"Probably not as surprised as I was," I muttered.

"At least there was one good thing to come out of that bumpy as hell wormhole," he commented while eyeing my butt again as if to enact a charade of just what that *one good thing* was.

"You're so predictable, you're beginning to bore me," I said with my nose in the air.

"Leave the next twenty minutes up to me and we'll see how bored you are."

I just looked at him blankly before expelling an exasperated sigh. "Ugh, you're a pain in my butt whether you're locked up or free, you know that?"

"Baby, I would like nothing more than to be a pain in your butt," Jax retorted with a more lascivious glint in his eyes. "A very large pain in your butt, I might add."

I chose to ignore the whole *large* comment. Instead, I focused on the fact that our most recent exchange was pretty much my fault. "Yeah, stupid me," I grumbled with a brief nod. "I set myself up for that one," I finished while backing up into a tree, thus preventing Jax's eyes from feasting on my rear any longer.

"Tell me something, has that boyfriend of yours ever had the privilege of ..." he started to ask, but I immediately held my hand up. With my palm facing him, I tacitly told him he could talk to the hand because the rest of me refused any part of this conversation. "Well?" he asked, obviously not able to understand sign language.

"We are absolutely not discussing anything else personal now or ever!" I responded, spearing him with my piercing gaze. I then wondered if my magic would work here, wherever *here* happened to be.

"Okay, okay," he finally relented. Holding his hands up, he smiled down at me. "May I just finish by saying that your ass felt every bit as tight and round as I imagined it would?"

"No."

"You know, I think you have single-handedly turned me into an ass man!" he continued, nodding and seeming excited over the fact. "I used to be exclusively a breast man, as I told you, but now I'm thinking better of it."

"Great, I'm happy for you," I grumbled. All the while I hoped and prayed my magic would work now, because if it didn't, there wasn't much more I could do about my current state of undress. And that was a subject which deeply worried me.

"So I got a little peek at your lower assets but you've still given me nothing regarding your upper ones," he continued with a shrug. "How's about you take that shirt off and show me what you're working with upstairs?"

"How's about you give it a freaking rest!" I yelled while shaking my head. "Oh my God, you are beyond frustrating!" I closed my eyes and fisted my hand, starting to shake it in order to conjure up my magical dust but Jax's grating voice interrupted me.

"You probably didn't notice it when I caught you, but I copped a generous feel," he confessed, clearly ignoring my last comment. Actually, it was probably fair to say that Jax, in general, ignored nearly everything that came out of my mouth. He was exasperating to say the least.

"Yeah, I noticed," I admitted, opening my eyes to glare at him.

"You did and yet I didn't get a complaint?" he asked, smiling with true mirth. "Interesting. Should I take that to mean that you enjoyed being felt up?"

"No!" I railed back at him. "In general, it's safe to say that anything having to do with you and sex leaves me nothing but maddened, disgusted and ready to pull my own hair out."

"You say that," he continued, eyeing me narrowly. "And yet, I can't help but wonder why you didn't discourage me much earlier, if my roaming hands really bothered you that much." His eyebrows reached for the tops of the trees as he shook my head. "Methinks the truth is more along the lines of you wanting me as much as I want you."

"No," I insisted immediately. "The truth is more along the lines of me being so shocked by everything that I'd just gone through that I wasn't paying enough attention to you and your attempts to molest me. Had I been completely coherent, your hand would now be broken."

"Well, that, or we'd be pursuing other, more pleasurable activities," he purred with a look of unrestrained hunger again.

But I wasn't paying him any attention because I was too busy trying to magick myself a pair of pants. Closing my eyes again, I silently prayed my magic would work as I shook my right hand. A few seconds later, I felt a mound of my dust materialize in my palm. *Things were looking up ...*

I opened my eyes when I threw the magical particles directly over my head. As I watched the glittery specks sprinkling down on top of me, I imagined a pair of jeans covering my lower half. Seconds later, I smiled to see I was no longer naked from the waist down, but clad in my favorite Levis.

"And just when I was beginning to really appreciate the view," Jax said with a frown while shaking his head and acting overly disappointed.

"Okay! That's enough," I sniped back at him. Taking a deep breath, I tried to figure out a plan, something to keep me moving forward. First of all, however, I needed to understand what had just happened to us over the last ten minutes or so.

"I'm not sure which is worse—grabbing a healthy feel of your ass, or never having had the opportunity in the first place," he lamented in dramatic soliloquy.

"I don't care."

"I know the answer," he continued, nodding. "It's worse now that I've had the opportunity," he finished, obviously ignoring my comment. He might as well have been having the conversation with himself. "Only because now I can't stop thinking about getting another feel."

"Oh, my God, you are so exhausting," I replied with my hands on my hips as I shook my head in pure desperation. "I have no energy left to deal with you anymore."

"You don't know the half of how exhausting I can be, baby girl," he answered with a wink that made me want to vomit.

"I don't want to know the half of it! I don't want to know a third of it! I don't want to know any of it!" I barked, taking a deep breath before entering the more important conversation that we still needed to have. "What I do want to know, however, is what happened back there?"

"What happened back … where?"

My heartrate increased again, but this time, out of growing frustration. "Oh, I don't know, for starters, how about us both disappearing into the wormhole?"

He shrugged. "Sounds like you summed the whole thing up fairly well. What more would you like to know?"

"Don't screw around with me, Jax!" I yelled at him finally, feeling my temper starting to fray. "I'm not in the mood for it!" Then I inhaled deeply three times because I was suddenly feeling faint.

"I would never try to screw around with you, Dulcie," he answered, that pesky smile of his in full effect.

My heartbeat started to pound through my chest again; and despite some more deep breaths to slow it down, it persisted. I felt like I was on overload at the moment. I had no clue what had happened to me, much less where I was. Furthermore, I wondered if there was any way back—was I even still traveling on an Earthly plane? I figured I must have been because my magic worked here; and it didn't in the Netherworld. Throwing Jax into the mix was just one more question mark and one more answer I didn't have.

I decided to sit down for a second or two until I could get my fight or flight response under control. Putting my head between my knees, I closed my eyes.

You can handle this, Dulce, I told myself. *You're tough and strong and you can handle whatever curveball life might throw at you. All you need is a little bit of downtime, just enough so you can catch your breath and think more clearly.*

"This is good training for you," Jax interjected.

"I don't need more training," I muttered in reply. I failed to suppress my scowl as I glanced up at him briefly before wedging my head between my knees again.

"All good recruits never stop training," he continued, commanding my attention again as he shrugged, like I should have admitted that he had a point.

"I'm not a recruit!" I yelled in a moment of unrestrained frustration. Yes, I realized almost instantly that it was a bad move. I shouldn't have been ready to reveal my cards at this point, but I couldn't say I cared anymore. I just wanted to get him to shut the hell up.

"You're not a recruit?" he asked, shaking his head. Then he *tsked* me, but didn't seem really offended. "It appears the honorable ANC officer hasn't been exactly straight with me."

"No, I haven't been," I answered with no trace of apology. Then I laughed angrily. "Why should I be? It's not like you've been straight with me."

"Then we are at an impasse, aren't we?" he asked. His serpentine smile indicated how much he enjoyed our verbal sparring. But I wished he'd just keep quiet so I could formulate a plan in my mind to get out of this predicament.

"There doesn't have to be any impasse," I answered. "Instead, you could start answering my questions, now that you have nothing more to lose."

"You think I have nothing more to lose?" he asked, eyeing me with keen interest.

I shrugged. "You aren't locked up anymore, and you seem to know where we are, although I don't, and you're physically much stronger than I am, and I'm unarmed. I'd say you have nothing more to lose."

"Good points, all of them," he admitted with a curt nod. Then he shrugged. "Okay, ask away, fair lady."

"You've known exactly what was happening all along, didn't you?" I inquired instantly, sitting up straight as soon as I wondered if he might be willing to give me the elusive answers to my questions I'd been seeking all along.

"What do you think?" he asked with little interest. His expression showed the same lack of concern or surprise as he did when the "earthquake" first started. I suddenly remembered how throughout that episode, and right up until the point when he finally dropped down into the tunnel, his expression never changed.

"I think you had it all planned."

"Yes," he answered unapologetically. "It was all part of my sinister master plan," he added with a drawn-out, well-practiced, malevolent laugh that sounded purposefully evil. "And if it hadn't been for you meddling kids, I might have actually pulled it off!" he finished, quoting every ridiculous villain ever to appear on Scooby-Doo.

"So what was the point of it all?" I asked as I faced him squarely. My breathing had returned to normal, and the fuzzy feeling behind my eyes was dissipating rapidly. Things were definitely looking up.

"To get you away from Headquarters," he answered with a shrug, like it should have been obvious to me.

"Why?" I asked while heaving myself onto my feet. I took a few seconds to make sure I wouldn't get dizzy again and keel over.

"Because those were my orders."

"Orders? From whom?" I demanded.

He glanced up at the sky before taking a few steps forward. "I already told you—that's not your concern."

"I thought we were answering each other's questions now!" I retorted, wondering if I could ever get him to bend on that point.

"I'm only answering questions that I choose to," he corrected me. Looking up at the sky again, he seemed to be navigating by using the stars, which were now fast appearing in the dark blue sky. He glanced over at me again with a curious expression. "And I didn't realize we were answering *each other's* questions?"

"We aren't."

"You just said we were," he pointed out.

"I misspoke," I responded, shaking my head. "Getting back to the subject, since you won't answer that last question, how about this one? Was the sole reason you turned yourself in designed to get me away from Headquarters?"

"Yes," he answered without any explanation. Facing the sky again, he took a quick right, and walked forward a few steps.

"That doesn't make sense."

"You're the one who just connected the dots," he responded with a shrug. "If it doesn't make sense to you, ask yourself why."

"It doesn't make sense because I don't know your reasoning yet. I mean, how does turning yourself in result in protecting me? Especially when you had no idea that you would even end up in Splendor in the first place?" I inquired as I crossed my arms over my chest.

"Why do you say that?"

"Because you surrendered yourself in the Netherworld. How could you ever have known that Knight would relocate you to Splendor?" I shook my head the more I thought about it. "There's no way you could have!"

"Just call it an educated guess," he retorted before taking a few more steps forward and glancing back at me impatiently. "We need to get a move-on. It's getting dark, and those clouds in the distance look like rain."

"Educated guess? How?" I asked without budging.

He shrugged. "As soon as I told Vander about the death threats, he knew he couldn't keep me confined in the Netherworld. I knew he'd seek as inconspicuous a location on the Earthly plane as he could. And the one place that had to have been always foremost on his mind was Splendor, of course. That way, he could incarcerate me and see his girlfriend all at the same time. Sort of like killing two birds with one stone."

I couldn't argue because his reasoning made sense. Well, obviously it did because that's exactly what had happened. "Okay, so why did you take me away from Headquarters?" I continued. "Are you expecting some sort of ransom in exchange for me?"

"It's my turn," he said with steely resolve. "What's your favorite sexual position?"

"Really?" I asked, shaking my head, my frown in full effect.

"Really."

"I don't want to talk about anything sexual with you."

He shrugged. "Then guess we're going to have a quiet walk through the woods."

"You're such a pain in the," I started before catching myself and swallowing the remainder of my words.

If you don't play by his rules, Dulce, he's not going to answer your questions, I told myself and immediately recognized the truth in my own thought.

"Missionary," I ground out.

"Boooring!" Jax responded, wrinkling up his nose like he'd caught a whiff of something bad.

"Hey, you asked," I barked back at him.

"I was hoping you'd say doggy style."

"Well, I didn't. So, getting back to my original question: are you expecting to ransom me?"

"No," he replied while shaking his head and moving forward again. "And unless you start following me, I'm not going to answer any more of your questions."

I sighed with annoyance, but decided to follow him a little longer, just until I got all of my questions answered. "Okay, I'm following you now, so answer the question."

He glanced back at me, apparently to make sure I was behind him, and then offered me a wide smile. "I was told to get you away from Headquarters in order to keep you safe."

"To keep me safe?" I repeated. Now he'd lost me. "Why would anyone from a potions ring want to keep an ANC Regulator safe?" I demanded when the first raindrop splashed against my nose. He was right; rain *was* in the forecast. *Great.*

Jax shrugged as he faced me with curiosity in his eyes. "I can't answer that, baby. That's a question you'll have to ask yourself, or you can ask my boss."

"I have no intention of coming face-to-face with your boss."

Shrugging, he picked up the pace, ostensibly feeling the raindrops as well. "Then I guess you'll have to be okay with never getting the answer to your question."

"I guess so," I said with tight lips. "Unless you're just bullshitting me again," I slammed back at him, narrowing my eyes.

"I'm not," he pleaded with an expression of sincerity before wiping a few drops of rain off his forehead. "On this point, I'm being totally honest." Seeing my skeptical expression and visible disbelief, he laughed. "I thought it was weird to take you out of harm's way as well, but I don't question my orders, I just follow them."

I frowned at him, irritated that he thought I was so stupid to buy his ridiculous explanation. "Okay, let's put aside, for the time being, my opinion that your story has huge holes in it," I started. "And let's just say I believe you, for the sake of argument."

"Okay."

"So let me ask you what's going on that your boss would tell you to keep me safe in the first place? Keep me safe against what?"

"That, I can answer," he said with a wide grin. Eyeing the sky again, he began heading northeast. I followed him obediently. "But first, it's my turn to ask you a question."

"Ugh," I grumbled, having hoped he'd forget we were playing tit-for-tat. "Hurry it up."

He glanced back at me and nodded, his grin wide. "When a man's penetrating you, are you loud?"

"What do you mean?" I snapped.

He shrugged. "Are you loud? Not sure how more direct I can ask it. Do you moan? Are you a talker?"

I felt heat rushing through my cheeks as embarrassment stained them. There was no way I wanted to answer this question. Not when it was so personal.

So just lie about it, I thought to myself. *There's no reason Jax should know such personal information about you. If anything, if you make yourself seem boring in the sack, maybe he'll leave you alone.*

It was a novel idea so I ran with it. "No, I'm not loud," I said with authority. "I don't moan and I would never even dream of talking!" I paused to take a deep breath. "There, are you satisfied?"

"No," he answered.

"Well, I don't care because I just answered your question so now it's my turn again," I managed. I cleared my throat and tried to remember the question I'd last asked him before he sent me on this most recent tangent. "You said you were ordered to keep me safe. Just what is it that you're keeping me safe against?"

"Crossbones teamed up with a few other organizations; they intend to take control from the ANC," he admitted.

"Even though you swore up and down that they weren't interested in doing that?" I couldn't help grinding my teeth because it seemed he'd pretty much lied to me on all accounts. And now? Now I didn't know what to believe.

"Well, it's not like I was going to give away all my secrets to a cop who works for the ANC!" he rejoined. I didn't fail to miss the "duh" expression on his face as well as in his tone of voice.

"What's the difference between then and now?" I asked the obvious.

He looked back at me with a wide grin. "Now I'm no longer your prisoner," he pointed out. Even though he didn't bother saying I was now his prisoner, the hint of the comment hung in the air.

I chose to ignore it. "Go on."

"So Crossbones collaborated with a few hundred of our closest friends, and agreed the best way to ensure our desires and needs got considered in this new regime was by attacking the ANC from the back door."

"What does that mean?" I demanded, my heartrate racing again. I had to take more than a few quick steps just to keep up with him. And I did notice that he was purposely keeping his voice very low, specifically so I wouldn't tarry too far behind him.

"It's simple," Jax replied. "The ANC is so concerned about what's going on *inside* the Netherworld, they stopped worrying about what's going on *outside* the Netherworld."

"So?"

"So, if you'd let me finish, you'd have your precious answers a lot sooner," he answered with a lofty expression.

"Ugh, continue then!" I snarled, throwing my hands on my hips and giving him as much attitude as I could muster.

"I liked you better in your panties," he said, running his gaze down my front before frowning at me.

"And I liked you better behind bars."

He chuckled and then winked at me, as if to say, *touché*. "Apparently, everyone is focused on trying to control the potions industry within the Netherworld. But no one ever stopped to consider how potentially damaging it would be to control all the arrivals and departures of every portal that leads to and from Earth."

"So your plan is to take control of all the portal crossings in Earth?" I finished, hoping I understood what he was saying. "In order to ... what?"

"Yes," he finished with a curt nod. "To take the ports; that means there won't be anything traveling to or from Earth unless we deem it okay."

"So what?"

"So, that's where the true power lies," he explained. "One of the largest sources of revenue for the Netherworld is in its imports and exports to and from Earth. Not just contraband, but also automobiles, food, travel, you name it. If we control the ports, we control everything. Think of the profit! And that's without even including the proceeds gained from exporting street potions."

I swallowed hard because his plan made sense. It was well thought out. And it scared me to death. "And you think you can actually accomplish that? Controlling every Earthly port?"

"You've asked me a ton of questions," he announced flatly. "It's my turn again."

"Fine."

"Have you ever been with a woman?"

"No," I answered immediately, thinking I'd gotten off relatively easy on that one. "So you think you can accomplish taking over all of the ports on Earth?" I repeated my previous question before he could ask me another ridiculous one.

"I told you it was only a matter of numbers. And the gangs already have those numbers. Granted, we probably don't have the manpower yet, but that's just a matter of time."

"Until you can take over every portal from Earth?"

"Yes! And once that happens, we can work back retrospectively, returning to the Netherworld. Once we control all of the commerce to and from the Netherworld, we can determine what comes in and what goes out."

"Sounds like you've got it all figured out," I said glumly as I worried about everyone in the ANC in Splendor, and then everyone in the ANC in the Netherworld.

"Another big benefit in taking all the ANC offices at each port is that it provides us with plenty of weapons to use against anyone who tries to resist or come against us."

"I still can't figure out where I fit into this," I replied, frustrated. "If you intended to take Headquarters in Splendor, why not just take it? You had your chance way back when."

"Because that wasn't my mission at the time," he replied immediately. "My mission was to get you out of there before it was overtaken."

"Does that mean your people are in the process of taking it over now?" I asked. My voice cracked when I thought about Sam, Elsie, and Wally. The clouds overhead suddenly exploded with cold, hard drops of rain. They seemed to be reflecting the storm that raged inside me.

"I don't know," Jax answered in a softer tone. "All I do know is that I've got to get you out of here." As if to prove his point, he sped up his pace. "And I've got to get myself the hell out of this rain," he added. "I hate the freaking rain!"

When he said he had to get me *out of here*, I could only look around myself again. All I could see were the endless trunks of pine trees. Clearly, we were deeply ensconced in a forest somewhere. "Are you ready to tell me where we are now?" I asked, sounding hopeful.

"No," he answered. He didn't bother looking over his shoulder at me this time, but instead, increased his pace even faster.

"You do realize, don't you, that I'm not going to keep following you all night?" I asked. Throwing my hands on my hips, I made a point of staying right where I was. I'd already followed him far enough. And who knew where he was going?

"Suit yourself," he responded without bothering to slow down. "But you have no idea where you are, and the storm's coming. You also have no idea what's lurking inside this forest, because you don't know if we're still on the Earthly plane, or inside the Netherworld. Not to mention, you're also unarmed."

"So what?"

I could call his bluff on the Netherworld part since I was fairly sure I *was* still on the Earthly plane, or my magic would never have worked. The idea did cross my mind that maybe my magic could work in some locations of the Netherworld. Maybe it was like cell phone reception ...

"So your chances of surviving are much better if you stick with me," he answered with a shrug.

"I'm a survivor by nature," I replied while shaking my head. "And I'd rather take my own chances."

Of course, if I went my own way, that also meant that I would lose track of Jax, my prisoner. Not that he really was my prisoner any longer, considering he wasn't behind bars, and his compatriots were probably gaining control of Splendor Headquarters right now. That, and he was right, I was unarmed. It was probably truthful to say that I was more his prisoner than he was mine ...

EIGHT

It was at this point that I had a critical decision to make: either attempt to keep track of Jax, operating under the probably misguided notion that he was still my prisoner; or head back to Splendor to do whatever I could to keep Sam and everyone else I cared about safe.

It wasn't a difficult decision to make. I didn't know where Jax was going, much less to whom he was answering and, what was more, I didn't intend to find out. I knew enough about his mission, as well as that of Crossbones in general, to take that information and make good use of it. My only priority at the moment was to protect Splendor Headquarters.

Whether or not Jax would simply allow me to go off on my own, however, was another story. It was fairly obvious that he wouldn't. Especially since his express orders were to remove me from Headquarters and ensure my safety. Well, providing I believed him on that point anyway. And to make a long story short, I didn't. I figured the truth was more along the lines of Jax absconding with me in order to demand a ransom from the ANC. Why? Because there was no way that anyone in a street potions ring would want to keep me safe. Dead maybe, but safe? No.

I took a few more steps forward, in Jax's direction, even though I was still bringing up the rear. Luckily for me, the trees were so densely packed, the only way we could travel was in single file. At least it wouldn't strike Jax as strange that I was following him, rather than walking beside him. The last thing I needed was for Jax to suspect my intention to escape, or that I was now finalizing my plan on just how I could successfully do so.

The rain relentlessly pounded us with plump and very cold drops, but nothing appeared to slow Jax down. Ambling steadily forward, he proceeded despite the uneven forest floor, which was strewn with dead logs, sharp rocks, and piles of pine needles. Some of the piles were so deep, they reached my ankles. So, yes, I did lose my footing on more than one occasion, although I did manage to keep myself upright and moving ever forward.

Even though the going was tough, I was grateful for the density of the trees. They provided some level of shelter from the rain. Not a whole heck of a lot, but definitely better than nothing ...

Yes, I briefly considered magicking myself some shelter from the incessant rain but I wanted to conserve my energy and my magic since my escape attempt was going to take a huge toll on my magical reserves.

"I believe we are close to a road," Jax commented over his shoulder. He slowed down to a more moderate walk before stopping altogether. Glancing up at the sky for the nth time, he studied it for a few seconds, cocking his head to one side and appearing to be in pensive thought.

"Good, because it's cold and miserable out here," I replied with a nervous glance to my right and then to my left.

I wasn't exactly sure what I hoped to find, or what I hoped *not* to find, but all I could see were trees. The tall pines deluged the landscape all around us, with no break or reprieve. But if Jax thought we were approaching a road, I had to believe him, seeing as how I didn't know any better. Besides, a road going anywhere was very good news for me. Because I wasn't the star navigator that Jax was, the street would serve me well. I was hopeful that I could eventually reach a town and then figure out where I was. And, more importantly, how to get back to Splendor.

Every way I looked at it, the time for stalling was over. I knew what I had to do, and now the time had arrived to accomplish it. However, running away wasn't that simple. If I tried to beeline it in the opposite direction, Jax would run me down in no time at all. Although I was pretty fast on my feet for a woman, Jax would be faster. Of that I was convinced. But luckily for me, I had a little thing called fairy magic at my disposal.

Jax started whistling and then humming, the melody of the song something I vaguely recognized although I couldn't quite put my finger on it.

"...I want to feel you from the inside," he started singing and I immediately recognized the song as "Closer" by *Nine Inch Nails*. "You let me desecrate you, you let me penetrate you," he continued and I was more than sure his choice of song was by no means a coincidence.

I just shook my head, hoping and praying that I'd be taking my leave of him soon enough. I was even more hopeful that I'd never see him again.

"I've got no soul to sell," he continued, his pitch completely off.

Looking over at him, I noticed he'd already resumed his quick pace. The back of his head was now fading fast in front of me, so I immediately began following him again. I didn't want to give him any reason at all to turn around and check on me. And reprimanding me for not moving faster would definitely be a good reason. After he took another five steps without looking back at me, I figured he assumed I was directly behind him.

There's no time like the present, Dulcie, I thought to myself.

Fisting my right hand as inconspicuously as I could, I shook it once. Maybe my attempt was a little too weak, or too hasty, because I couldn't feel my magical dust taking form. Keeping one eye on Jax all the while, I shook my fist again; this time, with a little more gusto.

I had to resist smiling as soon as I felt the telltale sensation of ethereal dust filling my palm. A half second later, Jax began to slow down while looking up at the sky again. My breath caught as my heart climbed up and lodged in my throat and I wondered why we were slowing down. He paused several more seconds before turning right and resuming his quick stride. Like a dutiful dog, I obediently trailed him.

I allowed another few seconds to tick by, if only to make sure he wouldn't check on me. Then, with my eyes riveted on his back, I held my hand out in front of me. Rotating my palm, I released the glittery particles, sprinkling them over my feet. Then I closed my eyes briefly and imagined my shoes taking on supersonic speed.

When I opened my eyes again, I double-checked and saw Jax still forging ahead. Time was the only factor now, especially since I could feel the soles of my feet heating up as my magic took its desired effect. Taking a deep breath, I stepped out with my right foot, pivoted on my toes, so I was facing east, and broke into a full gallop.

Well, "gallop" was an understatement. I was moving so quickly, it felt like I was flying. Cold air rushed against my face, blowing my hair out behind me in a horizontal plane. I traveled so swiftly, I couldn't even feel the rain, although the smell of wet ozone tickled my nostrils, the scent natural yet clean. When I glanced down at my feet, they appeared as a blur, and the ground was no more than flashing splotches of green and brown.

After nearly slamming headlong into a tree, I reminded myself to face forward, lest I knock myself out and, thus, forfeit any chance I had of escaping. With renewed vigor, I raced forward, slipping between live trees and dodging the hulled out carcasses of long dead ones. After another few seconds, my feet began to slow down and I figured my magic was starting to wear off. Or maybe it was my body that was wearing out. Either way, moving at such a rapid speed was no treat for my legs, my heart, or my lungs.

The blurring colors on the forest floor started to delineate themselves as bushes and rocks. Pretty soon, I was moving at a comfortable jog. After my magic dissolved completely, I slowed down to a walk; but even that took too much of my energy, which was now beyond depleted. I had to stop and lean against a nearby tree as I strained to catch my breath. I suddenly worried that maybe I wasn't alone and glanced behind me to ensure that Jax was nowhere in sight. He wasn't.

Heaving a sigh of relief, I could only smile with amusement as I pictured Jax's expression of shock and surprise as soon as he turned around and discovered I was gone. Yep, I guessed it would be right about now that he was probably cursing and berating himself for not keeping a closer watch on me. Poor Jax ...

Yeah, not so much.

Knowing that Jax was no longer my concern was very liberating. But I couldn't celebrate it for long. Instead, my primary focus was figuring out where I was in relation to the road. An unfortunate side effect of my escape attempt was that I now had no clue if I'd put more distance between myself and the road or less. Hopefully the latter ...

Thankfully, my magic could also help me out of this predicament. After inhaling deeply, my heartbeat slowed down again to its regular pace. I stood up and took a few steps forward, craning my neck to study the canopy of tree branches overhead. I needed an open area, or a break in the trees, somewhere that I could observe the sky. I proceeded forward, but kept my eyes on the night sky as I tried to avoid tripping over all the forest litter confounding my path.

Taking another few steps, I noticed a small clearing in the trees that suited my needs perfectly. Once I reached it, I stood still and shook my palm until I felt my dust inside my hand. Throwing the particles in an arc above me, I closed my eyes and imagined myself floating upwards. Almost immediately, I felt a lightness in my feet, which could only mean I was levitating. I opened my eyes to ascertain my position and saw my feet floating about a yard above the ground. I had to smile at my own resourcefulness.

Impressed with my abilities or not, I needed to go higher. So, closing my eyes, I imagined my body soaring up as if I were on an invisible elevator. Immediately, the air rushed past me and I opened my eyes. I was now about halfway as high as the pine tree behind me, maybe twenty or thirty feet. A good start, but it still wouldn't do. I closed my eyes again, wishing to go higher, and my body complied. When I opened my eyes again, I was exactly where I needed to be—at the very top of the tree. Good thing I wasn't afraid of heights because I was floating in midair at least fifty feet above the ground.

It was exactly as I'd intended—I had a bird's-eye view of the forest below me. Now I'd be able to locate the nearest road. Of course, having nothing more than the moon for illumination, that task wasn't exactly easy. The rain could now beat down on me fully too, and my vision soon grew bleary.

I wiped the heavy drops from my eyes and face as I beheld all the pointy treetops of the endless pines. They looked like a sea of green, with no break or hint of a road. Turning to my right and then my left, neither direction offered a different view. It seemed like the trees went on for miles. As to the street Jax had referred to? There wasn't any indication of a road anywhere nearby.

Maybe Jax wasn't quite the star navigator he believed he was ...

Twirling around, I still saw nothing besides the ceaseless treetops of thousands of pines. Could I have projected myself beyond the road during my escape? I shook my head, trying to figure out what went wrong. I mean, yes, I'd definitely run at least a few miles after I'd left Jax. Maybe I'd even managed to go ten or so miles in the minutes it took me to ditch Jax. But even if I *had* covered that much distance, I still should have been able to see a road from my current elevation.

Just as I was about to give up hope and turn to Plan B, which I hadn't even devised prior to this moment, I thought I detected the faint glow of lights in the far distance. Narrowing my eyes, I attempted to focus on the lights, which continued to grow in intensity.

"Headlights," I whispered as my heart started to swell with renewed hope. I watched the lights turning to the left and then the right as the car sped along the road, and a winding one at that. Several times, the lights were eclipsed by the trees, but only seconds later, they reappeared. I continued to follow the light with my eyes, needing to figure out which direction the car, as well as the road, ran.

Turning slowly around, I watched the headlights weaving in a northeasterly direction. At approximately "three" on a clock, the headlights vanished completely. I had the answer I needed.

Closing my eyes, I extended my arms out on either side of my body. I waved them upwards and imagined myself floating down to the ground. When a rush of cold air blew from beneath me, I knew my magic had dutifully complied with my wishes. Upon my descent, the sting of a tree branch snapping against my face captured my attention, and I immediately opened my eyes and pushed the offending limb out of the way. Looking down, I realized I was heading for more jutting branches. In response, I swam through the air, trying to reach the original clearing I'd found, which was maybe three air laps away. Once I was freed of the tree's sharp branches, I closed my eyes again and coaxed myself back down.

When my toes touched the ground, I opened my eyes, and heaved an audible sigh of relief. The rain continued to pelt me relentlessly, owing to the absence of any cover inside the clearing. I took a few long strides to my right, seeking shelter from the forest canopy again.

Then I tried to figure out what to do next. Jax had to be headed for the same road as I was, and the last thing I wanted was to run into him. My best option was to try to hit the road at a different point than Jax would. Granted, I didn't know where Jax was located at present, but based on how far I'd come when I escaped, I figured traveling northeast was my best bet. And of course I'd have to stay hidden beside the trees, hugging the road's perimeter, rather than just walking down the road, itself.

My next consideration? Timing. Factoring in the location where Jax and I had been when I split, I figured we were pretty close to the road. Maybe only a mile or so away. If Jax had continued on in the same direction, after discovering I was MIA, he could have already reached the road by now. I briefly wondered if he had a car waiting there for him, or if he intended to walk, just like I had to do. Then another grave thought crossed my mind. For all I knew, those headlights I'd spotted could have belonged to a vehicle currently in Jax's possession.

Or not.

Since it was a question I couldn't answer, I decided to ignore it for the time being. Instead, I itemized the facts I did know in order to come up with another viable plan. The only danger at this point was in reaching the road and getting up close and personal with Jax again.

Calculating my present location, I conjectured the road at probably a good six miles away. Meaning, by the time I reached it, Jax should have already been way ahead of me, especially if he were driving. Or so I could only hope. Well, again, that depended on which direction he'd taken once he reached the road. I prayed he'd taken a left instead of a right.

But, if Jax was driving that car, he was traveling eastward, I thought. *So maybe it's better if I hang a left on the road?*

But what if Jax took a right and he's walking? I fired back at myself. *Then you'd probably run right into him since you'd be further east than he is.*

There's no way you're going to know which way he went, much less if he's walking or driving, I argued. *The best thing to do is make a choice and hope for the best.*

I eventually opted to take a right. Once I hit the road and headed northeast, it didn't matter if Jax also decided to head in that direction. I wouldn't risk walking right into him. And if he'd gone left and headed west, all the better for me because he'd be long gone by the time I reached the road.

Luckily I wouldn't have to rely on my magical powers for the next step in my plan. Instead, I glanced down at my wristwatch, which also served as a compass, with the click of a button. Pressing it, I found that if I continued walking straight ahead, I'd be heading northeast.

"Sounds good to me," I whispered before starting on my way again.

An image of Knight suddenly unfolded before my eyes as I wondered what he was doing at this very moment; and if Sam had managed to reach him and inform him about my disappearance. Then again, for all Sam knew, I could be dead. Actually, that was probably exactly what she would have thought since the last time she'd seen me, I was getting sucked down into a black pit.

The urge to reach out to Sam and Knight, just to let them know that I was still alive, suddenly overcame me. I ached to tell them I was lost in a forest somewhere, but still very much alive. But then I realized how completely impossible that was, since I had no phone. Unfortunately for me, my cell phone had met its maker when the wormhole sucked my pants right off me and with them, my mobile phone. Even if I managed to find another phone, in whatever town I might stumble upon, it wasn't like I could just call the Netherworld. Nope. The only way to make contact with the Netherworld was through special, ANC-provided telephones.

And Sam might not be alive anymore, Dulcie, that small voice in my head suddenly piped up. It was a thought I had to instantly banish. There was no way I would allow myself to ponder whether or not Sam was wounded, or dead. No, I had to maintain my unflagging hope. Without hope, there would be no reason to push harder. Hope was the only thing I had worth fighting for.

But the reality of what could have been happening in Splendor weighed very heavily on me, all the same. If what Jax had said was true and Crossbones intended to lay siege to Splendor Headquarters, or if they were already in the midst of it, the safety of my friends was definitely at stake. I couldn't imagine the potions rings giving a flying crap about Sam's life, or Elsie's, or anyone else's, for that matter.

The plan devised by Crossbones et al. to attack every portal connecting the Netherworld to Earth was a very good one, I had to admit. The ANC was too powerful a force in the Netherworld, and no one dared to come up against it, especially now, when all the heavyweights (aka Knight, Dia, and Quill, just to name a few) were residing there. Entering the back way was really the only hope in hell that Crossbones had to overtake the ANC.

And, yes, it wouldn't be an easy feat for Crossbones to take control of all thirteen portals, which were located inside ANC Headquarters here on Earth, but it also wasn't a monumental task. Especially now that Crossbones was reaping the benefit of strength in numbers.

I suddenly regretted the fact that every ANC Headquarters located on the Earthly plane also acted as a portal to the Netherworld. It hadn't always been that way. In the past, the only means of traveling to the

Netherworld from Earth was pretty complicated. First, you had to ask permission from the Netherworld ANC. If they approved your visit, and it was VERY difficult to receive their approval, the ANC would send you a strata-hopping dimensional portal in order for you to reach your destination.

As a rule, no direct routes to the Netherworld from Earth existed. There wasn't an airport where you could conveniently board a rocket which would allow you to hop dimensions. The few times I'd traveled to the Netherworld were simply via a "portal ripping" device which Bram had given me. The device created a portal wherever I wanted one, simply by the ripping through the air. The other times I'd visited the Netherworld were with Bram, who had his own set of tricks up his sleeve, Netherworld travel just one of them.

Any migrations between Earth and the Netherworld were controlled by strict policies. Why? In order to maintain the balance. Otherwise, the numerous and various Netherworld creatures could overpower humans on Earth, which the human government wasn't exactly thrilled about.

Ever since we'd deposed my father in the Netherworld, the new world order had to be set up. And the powers that be decided to install permanent ports in all the ANC Headquarters so that the critical contributors, like Dia and Knight, could travel back and forth more easily. Naturally, every port was protected by ANC guards, and strictly enforced. However, if the potions rings outnumbered us, there was very little a handful of guards could do to maintain the safety of the ports.

"Dammit," I whispered after failing to notice an exposed tree root and consequently tripping over it. I was far too lost in my thoughts; I needed to pay attention to the here and now. I checked my compass watch and realized I'd veered off track slightly. Now, I was traveling more eastward than northeasterly, which was a problem.

Come on, Dulce, you've gotta stay focused, I reminded myself. *You can't help anyone, or do any good, if you can't get out of this freaking forest!*

And that was the truth. Feeling like I was reunited with my most immediate goal, I hurried my steps, skipping over the uneven terrain on the forest floor as quickly as I could. I was very careful to check my compass more regularly to make sure I stayed in the right direction.

To my huge relief, the rain let up after another few minutes. My progress was still relatively slow, and definitely sloppy, considering how the ground was either flooded or muddy. But I knew I would see the road at some point within the next six or so miles, and that alone reassured me.

Dulcie.

It was Knight's voice and I could hear it as clearly as I could hear the birds calling to one another in the trees. I immediately stopped walking and looked around, whirling in a circle to make sure I was alone. It appeared I was.

Knight? I asked in thought, even as I wondered if maybe I was losing touch with my sanity.

Are you all right? came his response.

I could feel a beaming smile suddenly gripping my mouth and not letting go. *Yes! I'm okay, Knight,* I thought back. *Are you okay? And Sam? Is Sam all right?*

When he responded, his voice started to break up, sounding like I was talking to him on my cell phone while traveling through an area with a bad signal.

Knight? I repeated, my voice starting to sound panicked. *Can you hear me?*

Yes, his voice broke through the static in my head. *But you're coming in and out. Are you okay, Dulcie? Are you hurt?*

No, I'm fine, I responded.

Did you say you're okay? he asked again. *Your voice is breaking up.*

Yes, I'm okay, I answered, and then added after a lengthy pause. *Did you hear me?*

Yes, he responded, his tone of voice sounding hurried but concerned. *You need to tell me where you are, Dulcie!*

I glanced around myself and started shaking my head as I realized I had no clue where I was. *I don't know where I am!*

Are you with Jax? he asked.

Yes, well no, I thought back. *I mean, I was but I escaped. I'm by myself now.*

Tell me everything you know before we get cut off.

I nodded, even as I realized he couldn't see me, and tried to organize my thoughts, tried to find a good starting point to explain the whole mess of a situation. *It was a wormhole which allowed Jax to escape from Headquarters,* I started. *It sucked me down with it too. And the whole thing was planned by Jax and his boss. So his whole thing about turning himself in to get out of the lifestyle was bullshit. And I still don't know who he's working for.*

None of that matters right now, Dulce, Knight interrupted. *Stick to the facts that will help me find you!*

Okay. After I got sucked down the wormhole, I ended up here in this forest. And I have no idea where I am, I responded as I glanced around myself again, wishing I could come across a sign or something that might give me a better idea of just where I was.

A forest? Knight repeated. *What sort of trees are in this forest?*

Pine trees, I immediately responded. *Very tall ones.*

Describe the forest for me, with as much detail as you can.

Um, okay, the trees are so dense, it's hard to see beyond them, but I do know there's a road and I'm heading for it. I saw a car's headlights on it just a few minutes ago. The road looked like it was a really winding one. Oh, and it's raining and cold.

Do you think you're still on Earth or in the Netherworld? Knight asked.

I'm pretty sure I'm still on the Earthly plane because I was able to use my magic to escape from Jax.

Good. How far do you think you are from the road?

Maybe a few miles. I'm not really sure, I answered with hesitation.

I want you to, he started, but then his voice cut out again.

Knight, I can't hear what you just said, I called out to him in my head. I didn't hear a response which caused my heartrate to increase. *Knight, are you there?*

Yes, he answered. *I said I wanted you to get to the road and then ...*

But his voice cut out again. I was so frustrated, I suddenly wanted to cry. *Knight!* I called out to him but there was no response. *Knight!* I yelled again. *Are you there still? Can you hear me?* But there was still no response.

Knight, I called out his name in my thoughts. *Can you hear me?*

"Ah!"

I heard myself wail out as something rammed into me. The force of whatever that something was was so intense that I felt myself being pushed sideways and then down. My feet flew out from underneath me and I was airborne for the space of two heartbeats or so.

I hit the ground so hard, I couldn't move. I couldn't even blink or form a thought. I couldn't even breathe. It felt like my chest was suddenly caving in on itself, constricting my ability to draw a breath or force one out.

"Apologies," Jax said, tightlipped, as he stood up and dusted the pine needles off his arms and shirt. It was a silly thing to do because he was also covered with mud. "And, thanks, by the way," he continued. "Your little conversation with your boyfriend led me right to you."

Dulcie! Knight screamed inside my head. Tears swelled behind my eyes as I tried to form a thought to respond to him, but found I couldn't. My mind was blank.

I tried to respond but I couldn't. I was still completely out of breath. At the same time, though, there was a fire that was burning inside me. I started to recognize it as intense anger—anger for being thrown off my feet and into the ground. But the anger was also reserved for the death of any hope that had previously existed inside me.

NINE

"So you were able to eavesdrop on my conversation with Knight?" I asked Jax after I managed to sit up and catch my breath. But even though my breathing began to regulate, my chest still ached like an SOB, and my head ran a close second. I pushed myself up against a nearby tree and leaned the back of my head on the bark. Closing my eyes, I attempted to avoid the dizziness that threatened to disable me.

"I'm a Loki so it goes without saying that whatever your man can do, I can do," he replied, and I opened my eyes to see one of his eyebrows arched in obvious irritation. "So, yes, I was able to eavesdrop on both of your telepathic waves."

"I should have thought of that," I grumbled, angry with myself that I hadn't.

I slowly breathed in for a count of four, and then exhaled for another count of four, closing my eyes and trying very hard to remain alert. Yes, I could have magicked the pain right out of my head, but I had an inkling that if I even tried to shake my fist, Jax would be on me like a werewolf on prime rib.

"Regardless, the point is you're caught," he continued.

Vexed by his cocky comment, I opened my eyes just to glare at him. When I did, I found him standing in front of me, with his arm stretched toward me and his hand only a few inches from my eyes. He was offering to help me get back on my feet. Help that I wanted no part of. After a few seconds, during which time I just studied him, he waved his hand, as if impatient for me to take it.

"You look like you could use some assistance in standing," he explained.

Although he was probably right, I didn't want to give him the gratification of admitting as much. Taking another few moments to deliberate while inhaling deeply and then exhaling, I decided I actually needed to accept the small olive branch he was offering. I doubted I could successfully get back onto my feet alone. I sighed in obvious aggravation and accepted his proffered hand. As soon as my skin touched his, he hoisted me onto my feet and studied me with narrowed eyes.

"I wouldn't recommend attempting to escape again."

"I wasn't planning on it," I barked back at him as I rubbed what felt like whiplash from my neck. Still feeling slightly off balance, especially now that I was standing, I had to use the tree behind me for support. "I doubt I could survive another one of your body slams anyway," I added with a frown because my stomach was still upset from the fall I'd taken. "And while I'm on that topic, you could have gone a little easier on me. I am barely a third your size, you know?"

"I did go easy on you," he answered with a shrug as he leaned against the tree right next to me and considered me casually. "Not my fault you fell so hard."

"Really?" I asked in obvious anger but then just shook my head at his expression of amusement, because I found this situation anything but. "So what now?" It was better to change the subject since this one only kept pissing me off.

Even though Jax was standing way too close to me, and scarcely five inches separated us, I couldn't step away from him. My head was still too foggy and I half-wondered if I might pass out or throw up. Yep, I'd definitely hit the ground way too hard; I only hoped I didn't have a concussion.

"Now we get back to the original plan," he replied before walking a few paces away from the tree. I stood up straight and gradually released the tree, testing the waters to see if I felt steady enough to stand alone.

Knight, I'm with Jax again, I thought the words, hoping I could make contact with Knight again, even if Jax could overhear us. I just needed to give Knight any information that might help him locate me.

"It's useless trying to reach out to him," Jax announced after a purposeful yawn. Then he shook his head. "I'm blocking the connection between you both."

"Were you the reason we kept cutting out on each other?" I asked, frowning at him all the while.

"Yep, that was me." Then he shrugged, as if he didn't care that I was giving him the death stare. "I had to allow you enough rope to hang yourself, yet not let it kill you."

"What does that even mean?"

"Apparently you don't have much of an imagination," he started, his expression one of disappointment. I chose not to respond, so he continued. "I let you reach out to him just enough to where I could pick up on your trail, but I didn't want you to give him too much information, so I made sure I muddled up the rest."

"Really thoughtful of you," I grumbled, and then rubbed my forehead when I started to feel a dull ache in between my eyes. I took another few steps forward, tuned to my body to make sure any damage Jax might have inflicted on me wasn't permanent.

"You skipped a step."

"What?" I demanded with a frown. Although I wasn't as dizzy, which I figured was a good thing, my stomach was still sour.

"Crawling before walking, remember?"

"Really funny," I growled. Narrowing my eyes, I exhaled a breath of complete frustration. "You're lucky I'm not armed," I finished.

"Ah, come now, Dulcie, even if you were, you wouldn't shoot an unarmed man!" he laughed with a smirk while holding his hands up to show he was unarmed. "That's not the ANC Regulator way!"

"What happens in the forest, stays in the forest," I responded glumly as he broke into a hearty chortle. Feeling slightly better, I ventured another couple of steps away from the tree. As soon as I did, it felt like someone started repeatedly stabbing me in the knee cap. I immediately crouched down, cradling my knee until the searing pain morphed into more of a dull ache.

"Told you to crawl first."

"Thanks, but I could really do without your peanut gallery comments," I spat out before trying to stand up again. Once I was erect, I took a tentative step forward, more than pleased when the stabbing pain didn't return. The dull ache, though, was becoming more of a moderate one.

"You tweak your knee, or your ankle?" he asked, approaching me with sincere concern in his eyes.

"Knee, I think." I limped a few more steps away from him.

"Let me see," he said before reaching for my leg.

"Don't touch me! You're the reason I'm limping in the first place."

"Well, if you want to study cause and effect, you wouldn't be limping if you hadn't tried to escape *in the first place*," he remarked testily. Crossing his arms over his chest, he regarded me with ill humor. "So as far as naming the original wrongdoer, I would have to say only *you* fit that bill."

I took another tentative step, noticing with chagrin that every step hurt worse than the preceding one. "If you want to play that game, I wasn't the one who orchestrated the worm hole *in the first place*," I snapped, wincing all the while.

He cocked his head to the side and smiled at me. "Yes, you do have a good point there. I can't argue with you on that."

"I rest my case."

He heaved out a healthy sigh and shrugged, but continued to grin at me like the whole thing was one big joke. If only it were that easy ... "Guilty as charged, I suppose."

I didn't respond as I waddled forward, favoring my injured leg.

"At this pace, we won't reach our destination for another year or so," Jax grumbled as he came up behind me.

"Sorry I'm not exactly in a rush to get to my unpredictable future," I retorted before another shooting pain in my knee made my breath hitch. I sought out the closest tree and hobbled over to it, leaning on it to take all the weight off my bad leg. "And getting back to our destination," I continued, eyeing Jax as I started to massage the back of my knee, hoping I was just suffering from a pulled muscle and not something worse. "Where exactly would that destination be?"

"At this point, the only destination I'm interested in is the road," he answered as he glanced up at the sky and then back at me again. "And if my calculations prove correct, which they always are, we should reach it very soon."

"Okay, so once we reach the road, what happens next?"

He shrugged. "Then we'll have a long drive ahead of us." He started to smile again, and his teeth glowed very white in the moonlight. "Plenty of time for us both to get more ... acquainted with each other."

"A long drive where?" I insisted, opting to ignore his last comment.

"All you need to know is that you'll be meeting my boss, the kingpin," Jax finished. His expression told me he refused to discuss any more specifics. Or maybe he was just sore that I hadn't acknowledged the whole "getting more acquainted" bit. Either way, I couldn't say I cared.

"What business does he have with me?" I demanded, nervous to be walking into a situation that I was in no way prepared for.

"I don't know the nature of the business he wishes to discuss with you," Jax admitted as he shrugged and smiled at me again. "That, I'm afraid, is strictly between you and him but if I had to guess," he started, before his voice trailed away and he just looked me up and down.

"What does that even mean?" I demanded.

"That's one of those silent comments," he informed me.

"You're stupid."

He immediately started chuckling to which I just frowned at him and shook my head. The last thing I wanted to do was encourage him.

"It was supposed to mean that if my boss doesn't already have plans to nail you, he will once he sees you."

"I'm dreading asking this, but could this day get any worse?" I grumbled before taking a deep breath and trying to walk again. Not that I was successful ...

"You're limping," Jax continued, eyeing my injured leg with what appeared to be distaste. He was, no doubt, realizing my debilitation was only slowing us down.

"And you're an asshole, but you don't see me pointing out the obvious," I flared back at him. My eyebrows knitted together as drops of rain started to fall from the sky again, bathing my forehead, cheeks and chin in their cold wetness. Angry and indignant plumes began firing up within me as I berated my luck which appeared to have just gone from bad to worse.

"You're a fairy; so why don't you fix yourself?" Jax asked as he continued to assess my bad leg. Refusing to accept the pain in my knee as a legitimate concern, I continued to hobble forward. I took each step as gingerly as I could, but I couldn't deny the pain was getting worse. And it really didn't help to see the forest floor was covered in woodland debris, making it much harder to navigate without stumbling.

"You mean, I should use my magic and give you another excuse to attack me again?" I murmured as I continued to limp alongside him while he looked at me like he was afraid I was going to keel over any second. "No thanks."

"If you promise to use your magic for good, I won't attack you," Jax answered with a wide grin that was instantly lost on me.

"If I were to use it for good, I'd magick one of those flying monsters from the Netherworld and then I'd order it to swoop down and eat you. That or I'd magick a giant sinkhole to open up as soon as you took your next step and swallow you whole."

153

"So you do have an imagination after all?" he asked with a smile.

"Apparently I have a fantastic imagination where getting rid of you is concerned."

"Such a shame," he said as he sighed and shook his head.

"What's a shame?"

"I don't imagine your death at all, in fact," he started.

"Spare me the details; I'm already in enough pain as it is."

He dropped the smile and eyed me with what appeared to be real sincerity. "You need to heal yourself. You have my word that I won't try anything untoward."

"No offense, but your word doesn't count for very much," I rasped back. I was barely able to speak when the pain in my knee began to radiate up my leg and expand throughout my entire body. Irritated with his pedantic expression, I faced forward and with my jaw set tight, plodded on, albeit slowly.

"Well, regardless," Jax started in a bored tone of voice, "I have a schedule to keep; and you aren't helping me keep it."

"If you're looking for sympathy, I have none to give you."

"I'm not looking for sympathy," he quickly answered. "What I am looking for is a way to get this show on the road. And given your current breakneck snail pace, I'm going to give you two options."

"Two options?" I repeated in annoyance, without bothering to look at him. Truth be told, I preferred looking at the mud I was currently schlepping through. At least the mud wasn't a lying sack of …

"Yes," he answered with no amount of apology. "Option one is you heal yourself so we can hurry the hell up. Or option two: I throw you over my shoulders and carry you the rest of the way." He took a few quick steps until he was standing in front of me. "Option two is my preference because your ass will be in perfect spanking reach, which, as you can probably imagine, suits me to a tee."

"You never give up," I said, amazed that such was the case. "I can't even start to understand how you have the energy," I started.

But he interrupted me as he faced me squarely, and dropping his grin, his new expression warned me not to continue arguing with him. He stopped walking and clasped my upper arms, forcing me to face him. "I'm not a patient man by nature, so which one is it?"

"There's no third option where you get to go fuck yourself?" I asked as I scowled at him and my chest heaved up and down with indignation. The pain in my knee had become all-encompassing. With each beat of my heart, it felt as if the throbbing ache was invading all parts of my body. And it didn't help that the heavens insisted on releasing a deluge of rain above us.

FML.

"The only option three that would involve fucking wouldn't have me doing it to myself," Jax answered.

"Then I choose option one," I snapped, crossing my arms over my chest as soon as his attention dropped down to my bust. I didn't have the strength left to waste arguing with him anymore.

"Shame, I was hoping for option three; or, at the very least, option two, but beggars can't be choosers, I suppose." Then he offered me a radiant smile and all I wanted to do was sucker punch him.

"I'm still waiting for you to fall down a sinkhole," I responded.

"Sorry to disappoint you, baby," he said, his left eyebrow rising impatiently. "You've made your choice so get on with it."

I declined to comment, but closed my eyes and clenched my right hand into a fist. The rain continued to assault me with its freezing cold drops, making me suddenly wish Jax had a car waiting for him. Or, at the very least, an umbrella …

Shaking my fist, I immediately felt my precious dust filling my palm and leaking through my clenched fingers. When I opened my eyes, I found Jax studying me intently.

"And don't try anything funny," he warned me. "No running away at ridiculous speeds, or sprouting wings like you're back in the Netherworld," he continued as we both honed in on a squirrel as he scurried up the side of a tree, ostensibly seeking shelter from the rain. "And no turning me into a ground squirrel either," Jax finished with a knowing grin.

"The only thing I could magick you into is what you already are—a pile of shit," I said haughtily, my nose in the air.

"Ah, don't be a sore loser, Dulcie," Jax responded with another boyish smile. "All's fair in love and war, right?"

I didn't respond because my knee was aching to such an extent that all I could think about was healing it. As such, I held my fist above it before opening my hand. I watched the glittery powder sprinkle down on top of my leg and then imagined my knee acting like a magnet. In response, the particles immediately clung to it. Then I closed my eyes and imagined a bright, white light enveloping my injury. I pictured the light growing even brighter as it healed, working little by little to return me to my pre-Jaxed state.

I felt heat warming the area behind my knee. Pretty soon, it extended to the front of my leg and traveled to my thigh before returning all the way back down my calf, heating my shin and then my ankle. Once the heat dissipated and I could feel the cold wetness of the forest again, I opened my eyes.

"Good as new?" Jax asked, his eyebrows arching like my little performance must have impressed him.

"Damn it, you're still here," I ground out.

This only made him smile even more broadly. "You're too sexy for your own damn good." I didn't respond but lifted my bad leg a foot or so off the ground. Then I bent it, carefully lifting it up and down, back and forth, as I waited to feel any pain in my knee. "Good as new?" Jax asked.

"Only one way to find out," I replied, taking a deep breath as I planted my foot back on the ground and then I took a step forward. I took another few steps, trying to determine whether or not my magic had completely healed me. "Looks like I'm okay," I announced before glancing up at Jax who was studying me again.

"Good, then let's be on our way," he said with a quick smile which seemed at odds with how wet he was, completely soaked from head to toe. He took a step forward, but must have thought better of it, because he turned around again and reached for me. "Actually, I think I'll be keeping you a bit closer to me this time," he announced. He wrapped his mitt-like hand around my upper arm. "Don't want you to get any more funny ideas," he explained cheerily.

"You know what happens when women get funny ideas," I grumbled while shaking my head. Of course, I intended on escaping again, but at this point, I figured there wasn't really anything more I could do. Jax had already demonstrated his innate ability to locate me, even if I were miles away ...

Not that I was giving up ... As long as there was still breath in my body, I could and would never give up. As long as I knew Knight and Sam were still out there, I would fight my way back to them. But now wasn't the time for impulsive decision-making. Now I had to formulate a new and improved plan—one that was foolproof.

Now, what I needed more than anything else, was the luxury of time.

If there was one thing to be grateful for in this whole crappy situation, it was the car that was waiting for Jax when we reached the road. If nothing else went my way, at least now we had shelter from the incessant rain. The storm was falling in raindrops so big, I wondered if it should have been categorized as a hurricane instead.

"You should rest," Jax said as soon as I was seated in the passenger seat and he was behind the wheel. He cranked the heat up as high as it would go while turning on both of our seat heaters. I wasn't sure what sort of vehicle we were in—just that it was black and an SUV of some type. Not that it really mattered.

"Rest?" I repeated with an acidic laugh. Glaring at him, I crossed my arms over my chest because when I looked down, it appeared that I'd become a contestant in a wet T-shirt contest. "You abducted me, I'm soaking wet, I don't know if my friends are safe, and I have no idea where we're going, or what I'm going to find when we get there. And you expect me to rest?"

"You won't come to any harm," he answered, like I was becoming overly dramatic.

"Again, I have a problem putting much stock into your word." I took a deep breath as I faced the window. I couldn't make out much of the scenery. The headlights managed to light the trees a bit, but the incessant rain relegated them to nothing more than drippy blobs of green and brown.

"Suit yourself. We've got a few hours until we reach the portal that will take us to my boss. Then, I imagine, you'll find yourself very busy."

"The portal?" I asked, my nerves suddenly jumping to full attention.

I actually wasn't sure what startled me more—the fact that we were about to travel portal style or that I would supposedly be very busy once we arrived at our destination.

"Yes, the portal."

"What portal?" I asked, deciding this was the more important topic to focus on for the immediate present. "Are we traveling to the Netherworld?"

Jax chuckled and shook his head as he faced me. I noticed that look of amusement had returned to his eyes. "Which question would you like me to answer first, Ms. O'Neil?"

"Where are we going?"

"I already told you, I can't elaborate on that."

"Elaborate?" I scoffed. "You won't even answer it at all!"

"We are traveling out of state, but that's all I can say about it."

"To the Netherworld?" I repeated, although I was hoping and praying the answer was no. The Netherworld was about as far away from Splendor Headquarters as possible, and right now, there was no other place that I wanted to be than Splendor, if only to make sure that Sam and everyone else there were okay.

"No, we're not going to the Netherworld," Jax answered in a very matter-of-fact tone.

"That's a relief."

"Glad I could improve your mood," he jested with a wink.

"And we're driving to the location of the portal?" I asked, ignoring his wink.

"No, there's a horse and wagon waiting for us just around this bend," he answered. His eyebrows rose as we took said curve in the road.

"Funny, Jax," I grumbled. Terrible thoughts of what might be happening at Splendor Headquarters suddenly overwhelmed me. "What's going on in Splendor?" I demanded. I immediately regretted asking the question, however, because I wasn't sure I wanted to hear his answer. If I didn't like Jax's answer, there wasn't a damn thing I could do about it.

"I don't know."

"You don't know?" I repeated, frowning. Of course, I was more than convinced that he wasn't telling me something. "Come on, Jax, do you really think I'm going to do anything with that information?" I asked, shaking my head. "What could I possibly do when I'm basically your prisoner?"

"I don't know of anything you could do with that information; and yes, I agree, you are my prisoner. But that's beside the point, because I'm telling you the truth."

"Whatever," I griped and then brought my attention to the window again because looking at Jax did nothing except piss me off.

"You exasperate me," he said. "You must realize by now that not everything I say is a lie?"

"I don't know that at all!" I railed back at him. "And as far as me exasperating you, you have no idea how utterly frustrating you are!"

"Regardless of who outdoes who on the scales of exasperation and frustration," he continued in a bored tone, "I had orders to remove you from Headquarters. That's what I did. As for what's going on there now, your guess is as good as mine."

"Fine," I said, while crossing my arms over my chest and slouching down in my seat.

He glanced over at me, maybe to decide whether or not I believed him. "Did you happen to see a cell phone on me?"

"No."

"Right," he said with a nod. "That means I've had no contact with my boss or Crossbones since I was taken to Splendor. And since you and I escaped, I've had no way of knowing about anything except right here and right now."

"So why haven't you used that handy little Loki trick you exhibited during my telepathic conversation with Knight earlier?" I demanded, spearing him with a cross expression. "That would be the perfect way to keep in touch with your boss."

"Clearly, you do not understand how that ability of ours works," he started. "It's not just a matter of reaching out and mentally phoning random people. It's no E.T. Phone Whoever."

"Clever," I said with a grimace. "Then how does it work?"

"You either have to be within a few miles of someone or, in your man's case with you, there has to exist an extremely strong connection between you both." He was quiet for a couple of seconds. "Let me guess, he's selected you, hasn't he?"

I figured he meant the whole Knight's eyes lighting up bit. Not that I was going to divulge any of that information to Jax. "I have no interest in discussing my relationship with you."

"I'll take that to mean 'yes,'" he announced, but when I didn't respond, he continued. "Regardless, the point is I have no way of getting in touch with anyone, so I know as much as you do regarding what's happening at Splendor Headquarters."

"How very coincidental," I responded testily. I couldn't help it though. I hated not knowing what was going on, or whether I should be worried or not. All the unanswered questions hovering in the air consumed me, making me feel like I would lose my mind if I couldn't find the answers soon.

"I give you my word that nothing bad will happen to you."

I faced him with narrowed eyes. "How can you be so sure of that? You already admitted you have absolutely no idea what your boss even wants to discuss with me?"

He shrugged. "Because he told me that your safety was my number one priority."

"That doesn't mean anything," I grumbled, facing forward and slouching deeper into my seat. The seat heater was suddenly overwhelmingly hot. Or maybe that was just my temper flaring up inside me and overheating my entire body. "If he intends to ransom me, I have to be healthy. Otherwise, I'm not worth much to anyone."

"He's not going to hold you for ransom."

I faced him again and studied him for a few seconds. I was trying to grasp any clues from his body language, but he didn't give anything away. As far as I could tell, it appeared he was telling the truth. He seemed confident and calculating in his responses. Of course, that could also suggest he was simply well versed in the art of deception. "How do you know?"

He chuckled and shook his head. "You don't believe a word that comes out of my mouth, do you?"

"No," I answered honestly. "In general, I'm not one for trusting criminals."

"This mission was not about kidnapping you to hold you for ransom," he said as he stepped on the brakes and the SUV began skidding on the wet road.

"What are you doing?" I yelled while bracing myself for whatever was coming. Luckily, the vehicle came to a complete stop and we ended up in the middle of the road, rather than becoming up close and personal with the nearest tree trunk. "Was that really necessary?" I asked.

Jax's expression was full of determination. "My mission was to remove you from Headquarters, in order to keep you safe, and that's what I did. Those were my boss's exact words."

"And you don't think that maybe your boss was just pulling one over on you?" I asked as I scrutinized him.

"Pulling one over on me?"

I shrugged. The answer seemed obvious to me. "Maybe his plan all along was to ransom me, but he figured if he appealed to your great sense of chivalry, he could make you do his bidding without questioning his orders?"

"My great sense of chivalry?" he repeated before laughing and shaking his head as if to say he had none. "And what great sense of chivalry would that be?"

"I don't know," I grumbled as I wondered what in the hell I'd been thinking. Chivalry? "That fall I took must have really messed up my head."

"Why do you say that?"

"Because any man who body checks a woman half his size isn't exactly chivalrous."

"And any woman who thinks she can outrun her Loki captor deserves to be body slammed," he retorted

163

with no trace of an apology. "If you want to call a spade a spade."

"I'm starting to rethink that nap," I mumbled. Rolling over, I faced the window, trying to, at least mentally, emancipate myself from my companion.

TEN

I wasn't sure how long we were on the road because, amazingly enough, I did manage to fall asleep. Maybe because I was *that* exhausted.

Actually, there was much more to it than just my exhaustion, and the more to it had everything to do with Jax. I wasn't sure why, but something about him began to put me more at ease. Even though he was supposed to be a hardened criminal, he didn't now and never really had come off that way. At least, not to me. It was more fitting to say he seemed like nothing more threatening than an oversexed, high school jock. Well, an oversexed, high school jock with one mean tackle.

Moreover, I *did* believe him when he said his mission was to keep me safe. That wasn't to say his boss didn't plan to ransom me (which I was still convinced was the truth); but I also trusted that Jax thought otherwise.

Bless his misinformed heart.

"We've crossed over," Jax said in an even tone as I started to wake up. I stifled a sleep-heavy yawn as I opened my eyes, only to discover we were no longer being pummeled by the rain. Night still ruled the sky, but the enormous pine trees that had practically consumed us previously were nowhere to be seen. As far as I could tell, there weren't any trees at all.

"We traveled through the portal?" I asked, sitting up straighter. My heart started to palpitate when I glanced outside my window and tried to get a read on the terrain. I hoped to get a better idea of where we were, but all I learned was that we were on a very narrow road and we were still ascending.

"Yes, we just passed through the portal," Jax answered without bothering to look at me. Instead, he watched the road ahead of us, which was a good thing, given how precarious the drive had become. "We should arrive at our destination shortly."

"And let me guess, you've had a miraculous change of heart and now plan on telling me anything and everything about where we are?" I asked with renewed optimism.

"We're in the mountains," came his reply, and his self-impressed smile bordered on downright cocky.

"Thanks for nothing," I grumbled. Staring out my window again, I noticed myriad lights far off in the distance. They glittered from a valley ensconced between the mountains and appeared to be dishearteningly far below us. Regardless, though, lights meant there was a town nearby. And a town meant there would be people. I only hoped there would be people who would or could help me. Well, that is, if I managed to escape my current predicament ...

Jax stopped the car. I was about to inquire when I found we were parked in front of an enormous iron gate. He rolled the window down and studied the black box which would contact whoever happened to be inside the house. A few seconds later, Jax entered a passcode on the number pad before the gate began slowly swinging open.

"Guess we're here?" I asked, not able to hide the trepidation from my voice. I couldn't deny that I was nervous, because I had no idea what lay beyond those gates, which were now completely open. A well-lit driveway appeared, flanked by large trees that I assumed were some type of willow. Their long, hairlike leaves and drooping branches served as a canopy over the driveway and looked like they belonged on an old, Southern plantation.

"Don't worry; you'll be safe," Jax promised me again with a reassuring smile.

"*Safe* can be a very arbitrary word."

"Your physical wellbeing won't be compromised," he corrected himself. "How's that?"

"I'll believe that when I see it," I answered. I took another deep breath before we started the incline of yet another steep precipice. At the top of the hill was what I imagined had to be a breathtaking view in the daytime. But for now, the only thing I could see were the voluminous stars, twinkling in the sky.

"Come," Jax said, offering his arm.

I took one glance at it and then at him before shaking my head. "I can walk by myself. It's not like I'm not a revered guest here, so let's not pretend otherwise."

"Have it your way, but the cobblestones are uneven, and you *did* just injure your knee."

"Which, as you may recall, is now healed and, thus, no longer an issue."

"Just trying to help," he finished with a shrug before starting toward the house.

Well, "house" wasn't exactly the right noun to describe the monstrosity before us. It looked like the centerfold from one of those fancy home magazines. At three stories high, it had ornately intricate, iron balconies featured outside each arched window. On either side of the floor-to-ceiling windows were black shutters, a perfect contrast to the brilliant white of the mansion. The front of the house had no less than eighteen Corinthian columns, six on each level. The gingerbread cutouts that adorned the roofline imbued the building with Victorian splendor, although it was more fitting to say it looked like it belonged in the deep South. It reminded me of something I'd seen on *Gone with the Wind*.

Large oak trees hugged both sides of the walkway that led to the house, Spanish moss hanging decoratively from their great boughs. Below them were alternating bushes of red and white roses, all manicured perfectly, and probably the source of the sweet scented air.

Despite it being nighttime, I could see the landscaping before me almost as easily as if it were daytime. That was because of the endless streetlamps illuminating the walkway, along with the lights on the footpath, which were even more plentiful. The streetlamps, at approximately six feet tall, appeared to be constructed of black iron, and their glass lampshades featured etched angels blowing trumpets.

The angel motif was repeated in the fountain, which occupied the middle of a huge courtyard. This angel was very oversized, probably larger than sixteen feet. Her wings were fully extended behind her as if in midflight. In her hands, she held a bucket of water, which bubbled up and over the edge before running down her billowing robes and splashing into the pool at her feet.

"Someone must have a thing for angels," I commented, more to myself than to Jax.

"Yes, ironic, isn't it?" Jax agreed as he shook his head and raised his eyebrows, apparently seeing the irony.

"Funny, is it not, how a life spent in darkness results in the craving of all forms of light?"

The man's voice came from behind me, and in response, I instantly wheeled around, my body already poised in fight or flight mode. I stood with my feet shoulder-width apart, the best stance to ensure a firm equilibrium. My heart climbed up into my throat and every nerve in my body was alive and fully at attention as I searched for the stranger. But he was nowhere to be seen.

Seconds later, I spied the form of a tall man when he stepped out from the darkness of the trees and revealed himself in the light.

My breath caught. He was every bit as suave and handsome as I remembered him.

"Bram!" I said, my voice revealing my surprise. "You son of a bitch!" I roared as soon as the shock wore off and I was left with nothing but anger as I realized that everything I'd just gone through in the last twenty-four hours was Bram's fault.

"Sweet," he said, in a breathy, deep voice. "You are just as lovely as I remember."

"Don't *Sweet* me!" I yelled at him, even as I closed the space between us until no more than a few inches separated us. Then I did what any irate and justified woman would do; I unleashed the flat of my palm against his icy cheek.

If it were possible for a three-hundred-year-old vampire to look surprised, that's exactly how Bram appeared. He didn't even try to cover his injured cheek; but thankfully, it didn't seem like he intended to return the favor either. Instead, his long arms hung at his sides as if I hadn't ever slapped him at all. But this was no surprise. On the contrary, that was Bram to a tee. Eternally calm and cool, he was never one to lose his composure. And he was always dressed to impress. Tonight was no different. Wearing black trousers and a dark gray, long-sleeved dress shirt, he looked like he'd just returned home from the office, or was heading out to a nice dinner.

Of course, I knew better. Bram was a vampire and, thus, didn't eat food. And as far as any offices went, as the kingpin of the largest illegal potions organization, it wasn't like he was clocking in at a nine-to-five.

"I am rather disappointed, Sweet. I envisioned our reunion as a much more joyous occasion," he said in his signature, aristocratic, British accent.

"If I could drive a stake through your heart, I would do it in a second. No questions asked," I seethed at him. My jaw was clenched and my chest was rising and falling in time with my hurried breathing.

Bram was very tall—probably six-five or so, and broad in the shoulders. He had an overbearing confidence that ensured every person sharing his physical space had to notice him, and it didn't matter if the observer were a man or a woman. Seeing the perennial black stubble on his chin, cheeks and jaw, he again reminded me of a pirate. Well, pirate or not, no red-blooded woman, or man, could deny that Bram was handsome. Pitch-black hair and light blue eyes, along with a well-defined, narrow nose and masculine jawline endowed him with an attractiveness that any model or actor would envy.

Good looking and charismatic or not, Bram was currently taking up the number one space on my shit list.

"What the hell kinda game are you playing, Bram?" I snarled.

A mix of feelings swarmed through me as I beheld him—incredible anger since I blamed Bram for this whole mess and, yet, there was also relief to find him still alive. Well, not alive as much as still in existence. I hadn't seen or heard from Bram in several months, not since he'd helped orchestrate the expulsion of my father from office. Naturally, I'd wondered what became of him and hoped he was okay.

Also included with the anger and relief was a sense of gratitude because I never could have dethroned my father if it hadn't been for Bram ... Despite all those feelings swirling inside me, it was my anger that refused to be ignored. Anger because, as far as I knew, it was Bram who was the main threat to establishing the new regime in the Netherworld. But, more importantly, Bram was the reason why my friends in Splendor could still be in danger.

"What happened at Headquarters, Bram?" I demanded, still trembling with repressed rage.

"I must admit how I have missed your ... candor, dear Sweet," Bram said. He was staring at me like he'd never seen a woman before.

"What happened at ..." I started again.

"I'm surprised you know each other," Jax interrupted. I temporarily forgot that he was still standing there. Crossing his arms over his chest, he regarded us with unmasked interest.

"Of course," Bram replied. His big smile seemed to suggest everything between us was kosher and A-okay. "Sweet and I go way back, don't we, dear?"

"Stop calling me that!" I yelled at him and had to forcibly hold myself back from unleashing my fist against his face again. "Sweet" was Bram's pet name for me and even though I'd never found it particularly charming, now it irked me even more than it ever had before. And that's saying something, because I'd never been fond of the appellation to begin with. "I will repeat my question since you apparently failed to understand it," I snapped, glaring at him. "What happened at Splendor Headquarters?"

"She has a bit of a temper sometimes," Jax explained in an apologetic tone to Bram. Bram didn't reply at first, but kept smiling at me vacantly, and his eyes appeared almost glazed.

"Yes, that she does," Bram replied finally. The smug grin on his plump lips suddenly revealed his fangs.

"The only reason for my short temper is because you're a lying pile of undead shit!" I railed at him and had to consciously restrain my fists at my sides because I was seconds away from releasing them on his face and chest. It was silly, really, since Bram was a vampire. That meant he possessed unfathomable speed, and could easily dodge or avoid any of my blows in less than a split second. The only reason I'd been able to strike him at all was because he'd allowed me to.

"Sweet, please try not to get so upset," Bram purred, holding his hands up as a gesture to placate me before he approached me. "You must recall how difficult it can be for me to restrain myself when I detect a rise in your blood pressure?"

"Don't you dare come any closer!" I barked at him. "I'm having a hard enough time suppressing the urge to finish you as it is." Lucky for him that there didn't appear to be any stakes lying around ...

"My dear, let us not lose ourselves in histrionics," Bram admonished with a slight chuckle. Apparently thinking better of approaching me, he chose to walk toward the house. After taking a few steps forward, he paused and glanced back at me. He proffered his arm, suggesting I take it, or follow him, but I did neither. I wanted some questions answered instead.

"You're Jax's boss?" I asked as I crossed my arms over my chest and tried to regulate my breathing. First things first, I had to make damn sure I had all my facts straight.

"Yes, Sweet," Bram answered, almost in a bored tone. "I thought that much was already quite clear."

"And Jax's orders to remove me from Headquarters came from you?" I inquired, adopting my Regulator interrogation hat.

"Yes, Sweet."

"Were you also responsible for the worm hole?"

"Yes, Sweet."

"We've already been through this, Dulcie," Jax said, sounding slightly irritated, probably because I was second-guessing him.

"I want to hear all of this directly from the horse's mouth," I snapped before returning my attention to the *horse*. "Have you taken over Headquarters yet, Bram?" I continued, hearing the ache and worry in my voice.

"I believe that is the first time I have ever been referred to as an equine," he replied. The expression on his face showed more surprise than humor. "A snake, once, and a fox, although that was a century or so ago. A rat too ... Perhaps I have been called a rat more than once," he continued as if I'd asked him to elaborate. "But, never a pack animal. I daresay, I find the comparison somewhat insulting."

"Have you attacked Headquarters yet, Bram?" I repeated, ignoring his last comment because it was completely off topic and useless. Bram didn't answer me as he faced the megahouse again and started toward it. "Is everyone at Headquarters okay, Bram?" I called out after him. I raised my voice because he was nearly out of earshot, then I remembered how well the sense of hearing is developed in vampires.

He stopped walking and turned around to face me. "My dear, I refuse to engage in a shouting match to discuss any particulars," he said, shaking his head as if I should have known better. "If you care to conduct a civilized conversation over a refreshing libation in my drawing room, then I shall be most happy to accommodate you."

Of course, I wanted nothing more than to sit down with Bram and pry all the answers to my questions out of him. I knew one thing about Bram, however, and that was that he operated on a *quid pro quo* basis. In order to get what I wanted, I had to give him what he wanted. For now, I'd have to swallow my pride and stifle the impulse to stake him right there.

I didn't reply, but inhaled deeply before making the decision to allow him this small victory. I furthered my surrender by dropping my arms and approaching him. Jax stood right beside Bram and offered me a small smile of reassurance. Not that I needed any. Bram and I had known one another for years, and although Bram regularly straddled the line between obeying and breaking the law, we'd always enjoyed a tit-for-tat kind of relationship. In exchange for pertinent information and good leads, I usually agreed to ignore whatever outlawed antics Bram was currently engaging in. Of course, I couldn't say the same in this situation. This time, Bram had definitely gone too far.

"You've got a lot of explaining to do," I grumbled before joining him. He didn't say anything as he raised his brow and smirked. Then he led the way to the enormous house with Jax and me right behind him.

Upon reaching the double mahogany doors, Bram opened one and held it for us. Jax allowed me to enter first, and when I did, I couldn't help it as I practically gaped with awe when I beheld the plush surroundings of Bram's stately home. Smelling of fine Italian leather and hardwood, I noticed the entire interior featured rare species of dark woods in the extensive floors and paneling. All of the furniture was upholstered in black leather.

"Nice to see how well Crossbones pays you," I grumbled. Turning around, I faced the incorrigible vampire, waiting until he closed the door and returned to give us our tour.

"By now, dear Sweet, I would have thought you knew me well enough to know that I appreciate only the finest things in life," Bram answered without waiting for me to reply. "Please, follow me," he finished before heading down a corridor on his right side.

Having little or no other options, I obeyed him, fully aware that Jax dutifully trailed behind me. Not that I was worried to be sandwiched between the two of them. Maybe I should have been, but knowing Bram as well as I did, I figured I was safe. I only hoped it wasn't the wrong assumption to make.

At the last room down the hallway, Bram paused before opening the dark mahogany door. Like the two front doors, this one also was Shaker style. The drawing room, as he'd modestly termed it earlier, was far beyond impressive. The dark wood theme continued in this room but it wasn't the central feature. No, that was reserved for an enormous fireplace that occupied most of the far wall. The imposing mantel was constructed of rich wood that matched the front doors except it was intricately carved and spanned from the floor to the ceiling.

I felt my heart drop down to my feet as soon as I looked at the painting that hung above the fireplace. I was soon completely overwhelmed with a sense of déjà-vu because I recognized it. The déjà-vu immediately gave way to disgust.

"Oh, no," I grumbled before moving a few steps closer, and shaking my head all the while. "You've gotta be kidding me."

It was my portrait. I'd previously had the misfortune of viewing it a few months earlier, when Bram proudly showed it to me at one of his many homes, this one in the French Alps. After revealing the repugnant thing, he'd proceeded to drug me with his vampiric powers of persuasion and I'd nearly had sex with him. Luckily I was a fighter, and managed to break his control over me. Of course, Bram refused to accept any responsibility for the incident. He claimed he was merely testing my powers to be sure I was ready for our mission to banish my father and his militia from the Netherworld.

"Ah, yes, 'Fairy Law,'" Bram said, quoting the portrait's title. He gazed on it with the same adoration he'd had when he'd first shared the revolting thing with me.

"What's it doing here?" I asked. I was barely able to stomach looking at it because it was so off-putting.

"I consider it my most prized possession," Bram replied, his eyes firmly fastened on the representation of me in oils. "I found it very hard to part with, so I commissioned duplicates to be painted. They are exactly like the original and now proudly ennoble each of my homes."

"Un-freaking-believable," I grumbled as I looked up at the offending thing, feeling a sour taste in my mouth.

It was a full-scale rendition of me, and I was dressed in a very sheer, yellow negligee that left little to the imagination. The garment was so short, nearly all the flesh on my thighs was visible. The painting represented me with a sly smile as I pulled up the hem of the ridiculously short nightie. It nearly displayed the v of my thighs, making it appear like I was inviting the artist, or the viewer, to get *very* personal. And if the pose itself wasn't lewd enough, the perky, pebbled nipples that protruded through the flimsy fabric provided even more smut.

As for the title, *Fairy Law*, it had nothing to do with the painting. I looked more like a floozy from the

Renaissance Fair who'd been dropped onto the set of *The Sound Of Music*, owing to the background that included a meadow and all sorts of woodland creatures.

"It's you," Jax exclaimed with way too much interest as he looked from the painting down to me, and then back up at the painting again. I couldn't restrain the blush that instantly heated my face and neck. This was just so damn embarrassing ...

"It's not me! I had nothing to do with it," I insisted. Not for one second would I allow him to think that I'd actually posed for the hideous portrayal.

"It's very beautiful," Jax added as he glanced back at me and smiled even more broadly. "Though it's missing her...attitude."

"Yes," Bram said with a deep sigh. "That is the one characteristic that is most certainly lacking."

"That could be considered a good thing," Jax continued.

"Ha-ha," I grumbled at him in response.

"No," Bram announced as he shook his head. "I wish the painting possessed Sweet's fire."

I didn't reply when I noticed both he and Bram couldn't seem to pry their eyes away from my pornographic likeness.

"Okay, haven't you two stared enough at her boobs for today? I don't have time for this shit. I have questions that are begging for answers," I interjected, addressing both of their backs.

"Are those truly her breasts?" Jax asked Bram.

"No!" I railed in defiance. "Of course they aren't! Look at them! They're like a size F!"

"Sadly, no," Bram answered with another heartfelt sigh. "I knew Sweet well enough to suppose that she would never pose to have her portrait painted. Her likeness was created from photographs and my own impeccable memory."

I didn't want to visit the fact that Bram had photos of me or how he'd gotten them or when or why. Not when there were still too many pertinent questions weighing on me. I turned around and scanned the rest of the room, not wanting to waste another second looking at the horrible painting.

The furniture in the room was covered in a rich brocade of velvet, which matched the same shade of red in several of the Oriental rugs. And if the fireplace (minus the dreadful painting) wasn't the most arresting feature in the room, the ceiling certainly was. Painted a light vanilla shade, it included a bas-relief in a scrolling pattern that was repeated all across the entire ceiling. The room was definitely a study in overindulgence and extreme wealth.

Exactly like Bram, himself.

In trying so hard to concentrate on anything but the painting, it took me a few seconds before I realized music was playing in the room. I didn't recognize the tune, but it was soft, yet it also had a quick beat. It almost sounded like a mix between dance and electronica but with a much more chill vibe.

"Hey!" I yelled at both of their backs. "Enough with the painting!"

Bram was the first one who turned around and faced me with an apologetic smile. "It is far too easy to lose oneself in your inexplicable expression, captured here on the portrait, my dear," he explained. Then, eyeing the empty couch in front of me, he inclined his head toward it, and said, "Please, take a seat."

Bram sat down on a richly upholstered chair beside the fireplace, and I noticed there weren't any logs on the iron grate. "No fire tonight, Bram?" I asked, even though I already knew the answer to the question. A burning fire would make no difference to Bram. As a vampire, he was forever perpetually cold. Environmental conditions made no difference to him.

Sitting down on the couch across from Bram, I faced Jax, growing curious as to whether he would stay or go.

"Jax, thank you for accomplishing a well-performed task. I am very pleased to see you obeyed my orders meticulously and delivered her completely intact." Bram emitted a deep chuckle and winked at me.

"Of course," Jax answered. Taking one last glance at the painting, he gave Bram a quick nod before his eyes fell on me. "And you, *Sweet*, better behave yourself," he added with a flirtatious smile.

"On the contrary! One of the reasons our little spitfire enthralls me so is because she *never* behaves herself," Bram retorted while eyeing me with fond praise.

"Enough! I have no more patience for any of this shit," I interrupted. "Jax, if you have somewhere to go, then get going!" I snapped.

"Your patience is highly commendable," he said to Bram before frowning at me. Shaking his head, he started for the door, and his deep laugh trailed him all the way down the hallway. Once he was out of earshot, I faced Bram again. I had so many questions for him, it felt like my head was spinning. I didn't even know where to begin.

"Sweet," he said while staring at me pointedly, "shall I offer you something to drink?"

"No," I nearly snarled. "This isn't any social visit. In case you're suffering from temporary amnesia, you ordered Jax to *kidnap* me!"

"Ah, yes, well, let us discuss that subject in due time," Bram replied, and I immediately shook my head.

"No! We will discuss it right now. Why did you order me to be removed from Headquarters?" My eyes widened with unrepressed anger when something suddenly dawned on me. "And if you think for one second that I would willingly allow you to hold me hostage, just so you can use me as ransom for the ANC, you've got your head crammed way too far up your own ass!"

Bram immediately started to laugh even as he shook his head. "Sweet, Sweet," he crooned. "I would never think of doing something so nefarious and underhanded as all that."

"Really? I doubt that very much!" I roared hastily before remembering to control my temper and calm the *eff* down. As a rule, Bram always seemed more willing to work with me when I was in a calm state of mind. If I were riled up, he generally tried to push my reactionary buttons just to make me more so. And that meant we'd end up getting nowhere.

"Shall we leave the subject of *why* I ordered you to be removed from Headquarters alone for the moment? I daresay it is a long and convoluted answer," Bram replied. "I am certain there are other, more pressing questions you wish to ask me?"

"Yes," I replied, jumping on his open offer immediately. I figured we'd eventually circle back around again to the reasons why he'd involved Jax in the first place. But, for now, the most important subject occupying my mind was the question about what was or wasn't going on in Splendor. "What's happening at Headquarters?"

He studied me for a few seconds with a mysterious smile. "I apologize for failing to grasp the essence of your question, Sweet. Please find another way to restate it."

"Jax told me you deliberately planned to attack Splendor Headquarters so you could take control of the portal to the Netherworld."

"Yes, that is so," Bram answered. His candid response hung in the air for a few seconds because I was suddenly so angry to hear it, I couldn't even comment.

But I had to ignore my anger and outrage for the time being, I needed to learn what forces I was now competing against. "Tell me if you attacked Splendor; and if you did, then tell me if everyone who works there is all right?" I insisted.

"You must calm down, my pet," Bram announced, eyeing me with concern. "I believe you are near hyperventilating."

"I'm fine," I ground out and then taking a deep breath, I thought about Sam and wondered if she might be injured. "If you did attack Headquarters, you had better hope to God, or whoever the hell you worship, that everyone is okay. If not, you'll have me to deal with." I tried to exhale all the anxiety inside me before adding, "And it won't be pretty."

ELEVEN

"Do you recall that evening when I first revealed to you your portrait?" Bram asked as he faced me with his left brow arched in unmasked curiosity. "When you and I came the closest we have ever come to acquiring intimate knowledge of each other?"

I gulped down the huge lump that was forming in my throat as I faced him glumly. "Of course I do. I have nightmares about it every other night."

Bram threw his head back and chuckled heartily before focusing on me again. I watched him drumming his long, slender fingers against the armrest of his chair as he studied me. "I have enjoyed the carnal pleasures of many women, Sweet."

"Here we go again," I said before sighing in unconcealed displeasure. I noticed my knee was bobbing up and down, seemingly of its own accord. Usually, that meant I was feeling antsy. "Please spare me the details of your past sexual escapades, Bram, because I can honestly say I don't care!" I took a deep breath in advance of my next point. "And what's more, I can't even think about this conversation, or any others for that matter, when I don't know if my friends in Splendor were taken captive, or hurt, or if they're even still alive."

"Your friends are perfectly fine," Bram was quick to respond.

"Then you haven't attacked Splendor?" I asked, eagerly perching on the edge of my seat.

"I do not care to delve into those particulars just yet," Bram answered with a shake of his head. "Suffice to say they are all safe and unharmed. Their well-being should not concern you any longer."

"Okay, well, my next cause for concern is Knight."

Bram immediately glowered at the mention of the Loki and speared me with an unimpressed frown. "And what concern would that be?"

"I need to get in touch with him and tell him I'm okay," I insisted. "He needs to know that I'm safe and that I'm with you."

"I do apologize, Sweet, but that phone call will have to wait," he announced. "I must speak with you before you speak with him."

"That sounds cryptic," I said, eyeing him with suspicion.

"Call it what you will," Bram finished, his expression one that said he wouldn't change his mind on this point.

"But you will let me reach out to him at some point?" I asked, wanting to make sure he wasn't just bluffing me.

"You have my word," he finished before I witnessed a change in his thought pattern that immediately caused his eyes to dazzle. "And now I would like to discuss a subject of my own choosing."

"Okay," I answered with a quick nod. I assumed that was as much information as he was willing to give me about calling Knight and about the well-being of my friends at Headquarters, so I accepted it. I sort of had to.

Honestly, though, Bram had reassured me enough that I could stop worrying about Sam, Elsie and everyone else at Headquarters—at least, for the time being. And, strangely enough, I did trust him. I'd known him long enough to realize he was a man, er, a vampire of his word. So the good news was I could finally calm my fears, and that was enough for me at the moment. The not so great news was I'd now have to endure whatever Bram decided to discuss before I could get back to the truly important conversations. Again, I'd have to play by his rules.

So be it.

"Living for three hundred years has endowed me with all the arts and skills required to seduce the opposite sex, pet," he enunciated slowly, obviously intent on returning to this conversation.

Bram never had, and I imagined never would, give up on trying to have sex with me. Sometimes, I even wondered if it wouldn't have been easier if I had succumbed to his orchestrations. (Well, if Knight hadn't been in the picture, that is). If I had, maybe Bram would now view me as nothing more than a past conquest and finally overcome this bizarre crush he harbored for me.

He cocked his head to the side and appeared to delight in his own thoughts. "Or, perhaps, it is more fitting to say that my exquisite face and physique are truly the sources that procure me such a perfect record of success with the fair sex."

"Or maybe it's your incessantly long and boring stories?"

"Regardless of the reason," he started, but I shook my head vigorously and interrupted him.

"Come on, Bram, that was a good one! At least give me credit where credit is due!"

He chuckled briefly. "Yes, Sweet, you are quite humorous." Then he cleared his throat dramatically, and I winced to think he was again trying to theorize why his luck with the opposite sex was invariably successful.

Freaking Bram ...

"As I was in the midst of explaining, I have savored the willingness of many beautiful maidens," he orated, as if it were the beginning of another soliloquy. Still eyeing me rakishly, he continued, "And, yet, I can say without any doubt, in that exact moment when I held you in my arms and ordered you to resist me, even as you so willingly begged to succumb to me, that was the most erotic moment I have ever experienced in my three hundred years of existence."

I yawned on purpose.

"You allowed me a first glimpse of your most private sanctuary. You encouraged me, and begged me to thrust my flesh into your eagerly willing flesh, to penetrate you, to know you as I have known so many maidens before you."

"You're leaving out one of the most pertinent details," I grumbled while recalling the same incident, albeit very differently. My cheeks were burning with embarrassment, and I couldn't stop blushing. Sometimes Bram was just so direct, so blunt. Not to mention his bizarre choice of words ...

"Which detail would that be, pet?"

I felt my eyebrows climbing to the ceiling. Of course, he had to know exactly what detail I was referencing. "You were doing your damnedest to subjugate me with your vampire powers of persuasion. So whatever you think you saw or felt from me, it was entirely of your own fabrication." I suddenly remembered some of the particulars, and added, "And I'm still pissed off about it, by the way."

Shaking his head emphatically, he began drumming his fingers again on the velvet of the armrest even faster. Then, as if he couldn't resist any longer, he suddenly shot onto his feet and approached the fireplace mantel and the hideous painting of me. The tension was visible in his shoulders and the way he fisted his hands at his sides. He looked at the painting for a good five seconds before he turned back to me. When he did, he seemed to have gotten himself under control again. Well, his fists relaxed, anyway.

"I do not possess the necessary power to create feelings within someone that do not exist. They must already be there," he announced in a flattened voice. Maybe this wasn't the direction he intended or hoped our conversation would go. Not that I felt any sort of sorry for him ...

"Well, that can't be true," I argued with a frown.

"My powers merely allow me to unmask any feelings that already exist, and encourage them to emerge." He was quiet for a second or two as he glared at me. "But you already know that, Sweet, don't you? You just enjoy giving me a hard time."

"Although I have to admit that I do enjoy giving you a hard time," I started, since there was no point in denying it, "as to me having any sort of ... *sexual* feelings for you, I'm afraid that I don't now and I never have." Then I thought better of what I'd just said. "And I never will."

"We both know that is a blatant lie."

"What?" I ground out. My knee was now bouncing ridiculously fast, and I put my hand on my thigh in an effort to get it to stop. My fidgeting was making me nervous. Or maybe that was all Bram's doing.

"What do you fail to comprehend, Sweet?" Bram asked. He obviously mistook my outburst as confusion when it was actually mild shock over what had just come out of his mouth. "I am very aware that you harbor some level of sexual magnetism toward me. If not, you would never have allowed me the few liberties you did allow. May I remind you that I can only evoke emotions that already exist inside you. I am only able to stimulate that which you already desire; albeit deep down within your essence."

"That's bullshit."

"Perhaps you are not even aware of your feelings for me!" he railed back at me. "I daresay you have repressed them efficiently over the years, brainwashing yourself to believe you never ached for or wanted me." Nodding, he seemed to further contemplate the idea. "That must be so," he emphasized when turning toward me again. "Your pride forbade you to express your true needs, and you were forced to deny your cravings for me because you were and are too proud."

"What?" I started but he interrupted me.

"However, I released your inner voice, Sweet. I heard it even before you did, and I simply became your voice. I became the vehicle by which you could freely pursue your own deep longings."

It was my turn to laugh because Bram's ego knew no bounds. "So you think I wanted you to jump me? That's what you're trying to say in a nutshell?" I asked, my lips tightening. I noticed with some chagrin that my other knee decided to start bouncing incessantly too. I stood up, just to get my legs to stop shaking.

"I fear I do not know what you mean by me wanting to 'jump' you, but I am convinced that you yearn for me," he stated, in a very matter-of-fact and offhand sort of way. "I imagine you often lie awake at night, picturing the two of us naked and entangled. You imagine me on top of you or perhaps behind you and we are engaged in unspeakable acts. You imagine all of this until you can no longer resist your primal urges to impale yourself upon me and you must touch yourself in order to release your body from its prison. You have gone so far as to pleasure yourself while thinking of me, have you not, my dear? You ..."

I interrupted him before he could elaborate any further. "Let me guess; I've pleasured myself thinking about impaling myself on your ginormous staff?" I finished for him with an acidic laugh. His entire hypothesis was so ridiculous, it bordered on being offensive.

"I believe you often struggle while trying to restrain your orgiastic fantasies where I am concerned," Bram finished. The expression on his face suggested his victory. Well, only in his own mind, that is.

"Orgiastic?" I asked with a smile. "Wow, one dollar for your word jar!"

"The time is ripe for you to finally admit your true feelings for me, Sweet," he continued, with no amount of reserve. "Just say the words."

"What words?"

"Reveal to me how you crave me and have always craved me. Let us join together in matrimony of our willing bodies," he said, his voice raising an octave as it also grew louder. "It is high time we enjoyed the dance of our fused flesh."

I was speechless. For five seconds, I just stared at him in absolute amazement that he had so many ludicrous delusions. When I finally found my tongue, my voice sounded a little bit scratchy. "Wow, um no."

Bram's hopeful expression immediately gave way to a scowl as he glared at me for a few seconds. When he spoke, his voice was back to its normal pitch. "I am quite convinced that were it not for that barbarian to whom you so erroneously swear your undying loyalty ..." he started.

"You mean Knight?" I asked, just to be sure he was referring to *that barbarian*.

"Yes, that oxymoron by which the creature calls himself," Bram answered, his expression now of supreme disgust.

"This is great; I'm glad I have a front row seat," I mumbled, smiling in spite of myself. Sometimes, Bram could be so damn funny.

"As I was saying," he grumbled, "I am quite convinced that had he not entered your life, you would have surrendered yourself to my ministrations a long time ago." He paused for a moment and frowned at me. "And for that, I must admit I am quite resentful."

"Oh? You're convinced of that?" I asked, narrowing my eyes at him. Now this conversation was straddling the territory of starting to piss me off. "So you think if it weren't for Knight, I'd be riding the vampire train?"

"Indubitably so," he answered, although I doubted he grasped my reference. He glanced up at the painting again before clearing his throat and facing me with a pedantic expression. "At any rate, upon witnessing your unruly behavior on the evening when I first revealed your portrait to you, it only further convinced me of your desire for me. Perhaps, you desire me nearly as much as I desire you."

"Uh-huh. Let me play the devil's advocate for a second," I started, as I took a seat on the couch again and then leaned forward. I uncrossed my legs and then crossed them again at the ankles because I was tired of watching my knees bounce incessantly.

"Yes, do," he said with unexpected childish glee that seemed so out of place on the elegant Englishman.

"Let's pretend that Knight never came into the picture, or my life."

"That charade is not new to me, but one I indulge in nightly," Bram interjected.

"Stop interrupting me!" I railed at him. "And let me get my thought out before I forget it!"

"My heartfelt apologies, my sweet, please carry on."

Frowning again, I tried to remember where I'd left off. Bram always managed to do or say something that invariably frazzled me. "Okay, so let's say Knight is no longer in the picture and I did—" I started, but the words were suddenly difficult to say. I took a deep breath and pushed the rest of them out of my mouth. "Let's say I did harbor some sort of ... feelings for you," I nearly choked out, trying to keep the bad taste from forming in the back of my throat. I also didn't miss the smug smile that Bram pasted on his handsome face. He was such a pain in my ass. "Didn't it ever occur to you that any future between us was already doomed? I'm an ANC Regulator and you're the head of the most notorious potions organization." He just looked at me blankly so I continued. "Don't you get the 'duh' moment here?"

The smug smile he'd formerly worn began to vanish until it was a mere hint on his full lips. He stared at me, without saying anything for a few seconds, just appearing to be very amused. He glanced up at the painting again before sighing audibly. It was a silly thing to do, really, because he couldn't sigh, or breathe, or burp, or anything else that required a respiratory system; well, one that worked anyway.

"I fear our fate would be as star-crossed lovers, Sweet," he replied before turning to face me again. "Our romance would be thus immortalized, like Romeo and Juliet, Lancelot and Guinevere, Pyramus and Thisbe, Tristan and Isolde ..."

"Shrek and Princess Fiona?"

"We would rewrite the annals of forbidden love," he continued, obviously ignoring me. "And there would be countless books written about us, and songs composed in our honor." As a dreamy expression glazed his eyes, he insisted on staring at me, unblinking. "Dulcie and Bram: a love so tragic and pure, doomed for all eternity."

"Sounds catchy," I said with a grimace. "Maybe you can sell it to Dreamworks."

"I agree, Sweet; but fear not, our day will come, or our night, as the case may be," he finished. I figured there was really no point in me even being present for this conversation considering he was ignoring everything that came out of my mouth. But, like it or not, I still had to sit and tolerate it. That is, if I ever expected to begin the conversation I really wanted to have.

"We are an impossibility," I corrected him.

"Will you deign to explain to me why?" he inquired, his lips constricting.

"It's obvious, Bram," I answered, shaking my head because we'd just had a conversation, albeit a very dramatic one, but a conversation on this topic all the same. My patience was quickly thinning.

"Perhaps it is obvious to you, but not to me. It never has been obvious to me," he responded coldly before crossing his arms over his broad chest. He looked at me with visible displeasure.

"Didn't you just try to pitch me a movie about it?" I asked. Maybe Bram had lost a few of his marbles during those three hundred years. When he didn't respond, I sighed and figured I'd have to spell it out for him. "Didn't we both just agree that our job descriptions automatically preclude us from having any relationship other than a professional one?"

"Pah!" he responded before waving his hand at me and hastily dismissing my point.

"Um, wasn't that what you were just waxing poetic about?" I asked, now feeling completely lost.

"No!" he said before glaring at me. "You and I would be star-crossed lovers because I am vampire and you are fae," he explained, shrugging like I should have known all along. "Such an arrangement should never work as I want to devour you as much as I want to ... *devour you*," he said, and his eyes traveled down to my bust before dropping lower to the junction of my thighs.

"Devour me?" I asked with a hiccup of a laugh. "Hey, I'm up here!" I waved at him when his attention stayed on my happy place too long.

Eventually his eyes returned to my face. "I long to lose myself inside you, and become one with you."

"Okay, Prince Charming, I get it," I grumbled.

"Our careers in this life, with you as a Regulator and I as the Head of Crossbones, although on opposite ends of the morality spectrum, could never keep us apart," he replied. "They are trivial obstacles when compared to what could be our unending bliss."

"Hmm," I started, shaking my head. "Funny, but I don't see it that way. At all."

"Let us cast our caution to the wind! Let us ignore fortuna and the voice of destiny! Let us tempt fate, and see where it will take us!" he heartily suggested, suddenly wide-eyed and hopeful. I was waiting for him to burst into song and dance.

"I kinda think this is our destiny, Bram," I answered with a shrug.

"What is our destiny?"

"This moment right now."

"What does that mean?"

I shrugged again, all the while knowing he wasn't going to like what was about to come out of my mouth. "Maybe we are exactly where we were always meant to be," I replied, sensing the truth of my words. "Have you ever thought that?"

"I do not believe we are pawns of fate," he answered immediately, even shaking his head.

"Because you don't want to believe it," I scolded him and then added, "And on that note, I believe we have exhausted this conversation."

Bram narrowed his eyes at me, and a split second later, he was standing right in front of me. He stood so close, I could feel his cold breath on the tip of my nose. His unexpected appearance startled me so much that my breath caught in my throat and it was all I could do to swallow it.

"Confess that you feel nothing for me," he whispered. I was vaguely aware of his hands when they encircled my upper arms, but I wasn't sure if the icy temperature of his skin or having such close contact was responsible for the goose bumps that appeared up and down my arms.

I immediately closed my eyes. The last thing I wanted was to fall victim to his power and influence. "I could never allow myself to feel anything for you, Bram," I admitted almost sadly. "Even though you don't possess a moral compass, I do." When he didn't respond, I swallowed hard but forced myself to continue. "But all of this is a moot because I'm in love with someone else."

He was quiet for a few seconds, and I wondered what he was thinking. I didn't dare open my eyes to look and see if I could get a clue, though, because I didn't trust him.

"You fear my eyes," he said.

"Yes," I admitted, continuing to squeeze mine shut tight. "I don't want an instant replay of the last time we got into this situation."

"Perhaps that is wise. I doubt seriously if I would have the strength of mind I exhibited then." He tightened his hold on my arms briefly before releasing them altogether. At the sound of his footsteps, I opened my eyes and noticed he'd retreated a few steps. His back was now to me and he was again facing the painting.

I could finally breathe a little more easily.

"I must admit how I hate this constant combat in my mind where you are concerned," he said, and his voice was deep and low. "It exhausts and fatigues me. Sometimes, I fear it will be my undoing."

"I think you're being a little bit dramatic, Bram," I interrupted.

"Not in the least," he replied without bothering to turn around. He was quiet for a few seconds that seemed to drag on because I was at a loss for what to say or do. In general, I wasn't adept at dealing with emotional situations. And Bram was probably the most emotional man I'd ever encountered. I didn't know how to speak his language.

"Never have I known such sorrow as what I endured at your father's library when your life slipped away and I held you in my arms. The heartache, the pain ..." he started.

"Yes, well," I interrupted before clearing my throat. I wasn't at all comfortable with this conversation. I could feel sweat beginning to bead on my lower back and forehead. "I survived that ordeal, obviously."

It was actually a miracle that I was even here and having this conversation with Bram because he was right, my life had slipped away in his arms. After thinking I'd killed my father, he'd truly had the last laugh when he shot me in the back. The bullet had been dragon's blood which entered my bloodstream immediately and killed me within seconds.

I was fully convinced that I'd really died because I'd traveled to a place that existed beyond Earth and the Netherworld. I was sure it had to be the afterlife since I saw my mother there and she'd passed away when I was still a young girl. My mother, who'd told me it wasn't my time to go, insisted that I fight the poison flowing through me, and fight to live. So I obeyed her and did exactly that. I'd fought harder than I'd ever fought for anything. And I'd been victorious.

I don't know how or why I managed to defeat death, or how I was able to come back after being struck with a dragon blood bullet. They were notorious for killing Netherworld creatures in seconds ...

I just chalked it up to a miracle and left it at that.

"Yes, you did survive," Bram agreed, turning to face me over his shoulder with a sad, little smile. "However, the memory of that evening still haunts me, and refuses to release my tortured mind from its clutches."

I was growing increasingly uncomfortable as the seconds and minutes ticked by. I didn't want to recall my own death, much less the impact it had on Bram. Conversations like those were futile. All they did was frustrate us both, and for very different reasons.

"I never got the chance to thank you for everything you did for me, and for the ANC," I told him. It was a subtle attempt to change the subject again.

"Every action I have ever taken or not taken has only had one purpose," he stated as he turned to face me. His eyes were narrowed into an angry and determined expression. "That purpose is to benefit myself at all costs."

"I don't believe that," I replied, shaking my head.

Bram definitely strove to secure his own preservation, no doubt, but I found it hard to believe that every action he ever took was only to benefit himself. Not when he'd had such a huge hand to play in dethroning my father and in helping me, in general. And, truly, Bram had always been there for me. Not just in this most recent situation, but for as long as I'd known him. I'd always been able to count on him.

"Believe what you will," he announced loftily, "but my reasons remain the same. I am and always have been, purely motivated by my own self-interest."

"Then how do you justify your feelings for me?" I asked. I really preferred not to return to this touchy subject, but I saw no way around it, if I wanted to prove my point. "How do you rationalize your actions when they were specifically designed to help me?"

He shrugged. "Whatever I did for you is no different. It, too, came from a place of selfishness and self-serving."

"How so?"

"I wish to possess you," he announced flatly, and his eyes bored into mine. "Yes, I can think of nothing else but being inside of you, although there is so much more to it than just that. I want to *own* you, to know I can take you whenever and wherever I choose. I want you to *belong* only to me."

My eyebrows arched of their own accord because I couldn't say his response pleased me. Not at all. "I am not *that* type of woman. Nobody can or will ever own me," I said flatly. "I belong to myself. End of story."

"I fully realize that," he replied with a deep sigh before his attention fell to the floor. "Perhaps that is the foremost reason I desire you so much as I do." When he looked up at me again, his fangs were slightly indenting his lower lip. "Very little in this world exists that I have wanted and not taken."

"Maybe it's time for you to start getting used to disappointment?" I summed up with a hesitant smile and a quick shrug. I was hoping a little levity might lighten his somber mood.

"I prefer the word *Disappointment* to be absent from my vocabulary," he retorted with obvious irritation.

"You can't always get what you want, Bram," I replied. "Just listen to *The Rolling Stones* 'cause they wrote a song about it."

"Saying I have possessed anything I have ever wanted is not limited to material assets and wealth," he continued as he started walking toward me. "Every woman I have ever chosen and wanted has been mine, both in body and soul."

"And, yet, as soon as you get what you want, I'm sure you grow bored with it just as quickly."

"Yes," he admitted immediately, nodding, despite a frown that appeared on his face. "That is the irony of life, do you not agree?"

Wanting to finish this conversation so we could turn to other topics, I decided to try another angle. "Yeah, that's ironic but maybe you're looking at this all wrong?"

He stopped approaching me and paused, looking surprised. "How so?"

I shrugged. "I think it's pretty simple. Your desire for me provides you with a quest, a mission of sorts, something to keep you occupied. And something you find challenging."

He nodded as he studied me. It seemed as if he were trying to remember every part of my face. "Please, go on."

"Just imagine if I *did* give in to you," I proceeded, hoping my words wouldn't create the opposite response from what I was going for. "Imagine if we consummated our undying love for one another."

"I have imagined that scenario countless times," he answered, looking bored.

"But you haven't thought about it the way I want you to think about it," I barked at him. "So stop interrupting me!" Taking a deep breath, I only hoped my words would have the effect on him I intended. "What if, after finally getting me, or *possessing* me, or whatever you called it, what if you grew bored with me? Then you no longer would have a quest, or a goal. The challenge would be over and done with. And where would that leave you?"

"I could never grow bored with you," he protested, shaking his head as if I'd suggested something completely absurd.

"Just think about it for a minute, Bram," I persisted, since I didn't believe him for a second. "Everything is handed to you on a silver platter; you said so yourself."

"Nothing has been *handed* to me," he corrected me. "But I always achieve that which I pursue, so yes, I see your point."

"Has it ever crossed your mind that maybe your undying fascination with me has very little to do with me and everything to do with you not having me?" I inquired.

He quietly pondered the question, and continued to stare at me, but I could tell the gears in his brain were turning. When he finally spoke, he seemed more resigned somehow, or tired even.

"I do not have a ready response for you," he said. "This is a question which requires much more thought and consideration. I must admit, however, I do see your point; and it is a very salient one."

"And on that note, can we end this conversation for the night?" I asked, sounding hopeful. "I think I've been more than patient with you, Bram."

He nodded. "That you have, my dear, that you have."

"Then do I have your consent to shelve this conversation for the time being?"

"You do."

"And are you willing to answer *my* questions now?" I asked, praying for his affirmative reply.

"Yes," he said quietly before taking a seat in the chair he was occupying earlier. "But please, I request that you make haste. I must admit that my mind is elsewhere. You have planted a seed in my head that I find utterly fascinating, and now, I would like nothing more than to seek an answer."

"Then, I won't keep you waiting," I replied before taking a seat across from him on the couch. As soon as my butt landed on the rich brocade upholstery, I began my interrogation. "Why did you order Jax to abduct me from Headquarters?"

"Because I needed you."

"You needed me for what?"

He eyed me for a couple of seconds and then glanced up at the portrait of me. He studied the painting for a good while before facing me again. Without a word, he stood up and seemed to be totally out of his element, somehow. He seemed like he was uncomfortable. I'd never seen him like this before, so naturally, it gave me cause for pause.

"As you are already aware, the Netherworld is in a state of flux," he said while knitting his fingers together behind his back. He started pacing forward and reminded me of Sherlock Holmes. All that was missing were the funny hat and a pipe.

"Yes, I know."

"The ANC prefers one of their own to take the position as leader, of course," he went on, crossing his arms over his chest. "But the potions rings have other ambitions."

"I know all of that," I interrupted, eager for him to cut to the chase and get to the parts I didn't know.

"Jax?" he asked, and I just nodded. Bram smiled and shook his head. Staring at the floor, he continued, "Jax has the unfortunate problem of talking too much."

"Anyway," I prodded, anxious to get back to the point, "where do you stand in all of this?" A split second later, I guessed the answer to my question. "You, yourself, prefer to assume my father's role as Head of the Netherworld, don't you?"

"No, I do not," he protested immediately.

I narrowed my eyes and studied him. "Do I have 'idiot' stamped on my forehead?" I asked, shaking my head as my irritation turned to anger. "I thought we had enough respect for each other to tell the truth, Bram."

"I am telling you the truth," he insisted. "I have no interest in becoming the new Head of the Netherworld. I dwell in the shadows, far from the limelight."

"Then why are you doing this?" I asked, shaking my head because his reply didn't make sense. Well, only insofar as he liked to stay away from prying eyes. Bram was always a loner. And an ultimate mystery. It seemed his hand was in everything, but never obviously or specifically. And he always covered his tracks. It wasn't so much that he preferred to remain in the shadows as he was the shadows.

TWELVE

"I have never aspired to be in the public eye," Bram admitted. "I have always enjoyed positions of supreme power, but they were primarily behind the scenes, and never before an audience." He paused and took a deep breath, which was all for show. Then he smiled at me in that way of his that made me feel like the mouse to his cat. "I choose to be the puppeteer, never the puppet."

"That's all fine and good, Bram, but it doesn't explain anything," I argued with him, shaking my head. I wasn't sure if it was my imagination, but suddenly the temperature seemed to be increasing in Bram's drawing room. No fire burned in the hearth and I imagined the central heat wasn't turned on, seeing how little it mattered to Bram. I guessed it was just me. Maybe my conversation with Bram was causing my blood to boil …

"What does it fail to explain, my pet?"

"It doesn't explain why you want to take over all the portals connecting the Earth to the Netherworld. If you truly had no interest in assuming my father's role as Head of the Netherworld, what purpose could you possibly have in trying to secure all the portals? It doesn't make any sense." I paused for a second or two, but when Bram didn't respond, I continued. I already had a pretty good idea what his answer was. "On the face of it, it looks like the purpose would be to ensure that Caressa never gets to take her rightful place as Head of the Netherworld."

"I fear I have no alternative," Bram answered with a sigh, indicating he was bored with the conversation.

"That's bullshit and you know it!" I railed at him, angry that he had the gall to give me such a lame response. I'd thought he and I were beyond this by now. "Bram, the day you have 'no other choices' will be the day I find ogres attractive."

"Now who is being dramatic?" he said, a smirk on his lips. "And I trust at present you do not find ogres attractive. May I ask your opinion of vampires?"

"Vampires are fine and good, as long as they're telling me the truth," I snapped, spearing him with a determined expression. "And when they aren't being honest with me, they're better off dead."

Throwing his head back, he chuckled while I continued to eye him impatiently. Lucky for him that he was finding this conversation so amusing, because I couldn't say I was. Frustrating and infuriating, maybe, but hardly amusing.

"I do love it when you tease me with your sharp tongue," he answered after he stopped laughing. Then he took a few steps toward me, narrowing his eyes and his fangs lengthened.

"It's all completely unintentional," I replied in a bored tone.

"All the better," he responded with his eyes glued onto mine. "There is nothing more enticing than prey who never realizes she is being watched, stalked and hunted."

"I hardly consider myself your prey, Bram," I said with a frown before inspecting my fingernails.

"You are fae," he retorted with a shrug, "and I am vampire."

"So what?"

"You are the deer to my wolf."

I glanced at him, knitting my eyebrows together with skepticism to let him know I wasn't amused and, furthermore, that I also didn't agree with his comparison of me to a deer. "I am not now, nor will I ever be, anyone's *prey*."

"Perhaps you could prove your theory," he replied, his eyes dancing with excitement. "How do you suppose you would fare against me in hand-to-hand combat, my pet?"

I shrugged. "Pretty well. I have magic."

"And I possess extreme speed, tremendous strength, and the magic inherent in my eyes," he answered loftily. "Were our skills put to the test, I believe you would be outdone, captured and, ultimately, at my mercy."

"Well, here's to hoping we never find ourselves in that situation," I replied glumly.

"There is nothing more tantalizing than a chase," Bram replied, ignoring my previous comment. "And I can think of nothing more rousing than the thrill of chasing you."

"Speaking of the chase," I started, as I stood up, feeling exasperated. "Why don't we cut right to it?" His scowl was his only response, so I continued. "You and I have always been honest with one another—and that's the only part of our ... *bizarre* friendship that I've always appreciated."

"I appreciate many more aspects, it seems, than you do," he ground out, frowning at me all the while as if my comment rubbed him the wrong way.

"Regardless, the only way this rocky ... relationship can work is by both of us maintaining trust," I said. I walked around the couch and gripped the back of it, stretching my arms out as I pulled against it. Just dealing with Bram had put a kink between my shoulders.

"Do we have a *relationship*, Sweet?" The source of my neck pain asked, his serpentine smile especially flirtatious and, as such, especially irritating. "I admit, I appreciate hearing you refer to it as such."

"Relationship, friendship, alliance or a hostage situation ... call it what you will," I replied with a shrug. Standing up straight, I didn't miss the jolt of tension still cramping my neck and shoulders. "But whatever you decide to term it is irrelevant, the only way we can continue working together is if you're honest and straight with me," I insisted. "That's how I am with you. We both have certain expectations and obligations for each other that we must continue to meet. Otherwise, whatever connection we share will fall apart. We're skating on extremely thin ice as it is."

"I have cast away all of my expectations of you. You constantly disappoint me," he replied. Arching his eyebrows dramatically, he walked closer until he was only a few paces from me. He clasped his hands in front of him, as though he were preparing to take a casual stroll. With the backdrop of his drawing room, and the way he was dressed, he looked like some brooding, romantic hero. I had half a mind to start calling him as Heathcliff. Bramcliff ...

"That conversation has nothing to do with this one," I replied. The last thing I wanted to do was open up another discussion on his unrequited feelings for me. I doubted I could survive it.

Bram nodded after gazing at me for a few seconds. He thrust his hands into his pants pockets and took a few steps closer, but paused when he was less than three feet away. "I need your help, Sweet," he said in a soft voice, one that seemed more natural in a way, less guarded and more candid. Or maybe it was his expression ... Whatever it was lacked the artifice I was so accustomed to hearing from him.

"You need my help?" I repeated, eyeing him skeptically. "That's why you ordered Jax to kidnap me?"

"Yes," he admitted with a single nod before cocking his head to the side. He added, almost as an afterthought, "And I was worried about your safety."

"Why?" I asked while shaking my head. I wanted him to know I wasn't following him. I still wasn't sure I even bought the whole "keeping me safe" thing. It seemed a little too convenient, especially if he wanted something from me. "If you're the one behind the takeover of Splendor Headquarters, why be worried about me at all? There's no reason since you're the one calling the shots."

"Ah ... that it were so easy," he admitted, dropping his attention to the dark wood floors, which were mostly covered by expensive rugs. Sighing theatrically, his shoulders sagged slightly, like he had to support the weight of the world.

"What's going on, Bram?" I asked, not accustomed to seeing him like this. What was worse, I didn't like it. I was used to the self-centered, egomaniac who was self-assured to the point of cockiness. Then the thought occurred to me that maybe his woe-is-me act was just that, an act. Maybe Bram was just trying to manipulate me into feeling sorry for him just so I'd agree to help him. Yep, that was probably closer to the truth.

Rat bastard ...

"Bram, you need to explain everything to me—all of it in detail," I said after another few seconds, during which time he continued to stare, as if he were zoned out on the floor.

He brought his attention back to my face and nodded as though he realized the truth had to come out sooner rather than later. "It is not my preference that Caressa be outed as Head of the Netherworld," he started. "I believe the ANC must maintain a foothold in the Netherworld government in order to secure and enforce the natural balance of things."

"Then why are you doing this?" I demanded angrily. It didn't add up. I also sincerely wished he'd stop feeding me information piece by piece and just spit all of it out at once. But, of course, that wasn't Bram's way.

"Because I was backed into a corner, I had no other alternative," he said, sounding strangely tired, as if this nasty business was really putting him through the wringer.

"Explain."

"Those in the potions rings are very nervous about Caressa replacing your father," he finally divulged. "As you may recall, your father had a name and a particular *affinity* for running illegal organizations."

"My father was a backhanded, double-faced, son of a bitch," I interjected. My hands began fisting at my sides and my lips tightened whenever I thought about my father. My physical reaction was always the same. I hated the man when he lived, and I hated his memory now. "He was probably as crooked as they come."

"We both agree your father was what he was," Bram concurred, "and we both saw the reasons he had to be removed from office. Let us, for the moment, abandon our perspectives, my dear, and try to adopt those of the leaders of the potions rings."

"They probably loved my father," I admitted with a scowl before walking over to the couch and taking a seat. I folded one of my legs underneath me and focused on Bram, hoping this conversation would pick up its pace.

"Love, perhaps, is not the right word," Bram corrected me, as he nodded all the same. "Your father was very much feared, and I can say without any equivocation, he was a most respected man."

"Anyone who respected my father was a complete fool."

"The point, my dear, beautiful fairy, is this: your father was a man in *their* court. His own personal interests were well aligned and tied to theirs."

"Right, because he was profiting from the illegal potions market!" I railed angrily. My knee started to hurt so I stood up, only to sit down again, planting both of my feet firmly on the floor. "Yes, he was a hypocrite and a traitor since he also sat behind an ANC desk."

"Caressa, as you are well aware, is not one of them," Bram said, nodding his agreement. "To the exporters, as I affectionately refer to them," he started before I interrupted him.

"You mean as you affectionately refer to yourself?" I crossed my arms over my chest because I was growing even angrier when I reminded myself of how deep Bram's betrayal really ran.

"I am not *them*," he replied curtly with a simple smile that suggested he really believed his words.

"You're the head of the largest street potions organization," I argued, my eyebrows furrowed in irritation. There was no way he could ever convince me he was innocent in all of this. "How can you deny being one of them? You're their freaking ring leader!"

"That may be true," he admitted while shaking his head. "But I am not cut from the same cloth. As I told you earlier, I am the puppeteer; and they are all mere puppets. None of them see the larger picture. They only see the things I allow them to view."

"You're one and the same, Bram," I interrupted and considered him with a frown that said his overinflated ego wasn't exactly charming. "You say *ta-may-to* and I say *tah-mah-to*," I quipped.

"I do not view it the same way you do," he argued.

"Regardless, I'd rather you got back to the point."

"As you wish," he answered with another frown. As he approached the far end of the room, I suddenly noticed a white statue. I wasn't sure how I'd missed it before, considering how tall it was—probably the same height as I was. Romanesque in style, it was in the shape of a naked woman. Her hair was done in a chignon, piled on top of her head, although quite a few tendrils framed her face. Carrying a jug over one of her shapely shoulders, she didn't wear any clothes and her feet were bare.

Bram just stood there as if transfixed by the sight of her, his eyes following the contours of her body.

"Bram!" I yelled, clapping my hands a few times to get his attention. "What is it with you and naked artifacts?"

"I cannot deny my appreciation for the human female body," he answered, but then thought better of it when he added: "or the female fae body," and offered me a wink. "The female is the essence of pure beauty," he remarked. Shifting his head, he followed the curvaceous lines of the exquisite statue. "Every curve, every junction, every valley and every peak are the epitome of pristine perfection."

"Well, excuse me, but we *were* having a conversation, you know?" I was becoming increasingly convinced that Bram must be suffering from ADHD.

Sparing a glance over his shoulder at me, and showing little interest, he curtly nodded with a sigh. "As I was saying, the exporters do not consider Caressa their friend," he said, turning to fully face me and looking slightly despondent over that fact.

"Because she will insist that the laws be upheld," I deduced. Jutting my chin into the air, like I usually did when I felt self-righteous, I added, "Just like I would."

"Yes, my little warrior, just like you would," he iterated with a hearty chuckle. He studied me for a few more seconds before returning his attention exclusively to the statue beside him. "I must say, her body quite resembles yours," he said as he glanced from me to the statue and back again.

"Not interested."

"Unfortunate. The only conversation you seem intent on pursuing is the one we were just having," he replied with deliberate ennui as he shook his head.

Nodding, I launched right back into it. "I'm not stupid, Bram. Of course, I understand the reasons why the potions rings don't want Caressa replacing my father," I began, shaking my head. "But I still don't understand why you don't."

He nodded and said nothing for a few seconds as he apparently considered my question. Or maybe he was just buying more time to ogle the bare nipples of the statue. Actually, the latter scenario was probably closer to the truth ... I often wondered if maybe Bram had sexual problems, or could have been a sex addict. Shrugging, I figured I'd probably never know the answer, although the thought of it was a bit comical.

So this vampire who's also a sex addict, walks into a bar ...

"I support Caressa's right to replace your father because I believe there needs to exist a balance in all things, a yin to the yang," he announced as he lifted his index finger and ran it down the statue's cheek. "The Romans certainly had a talent for capturing magnificence in a piece of stone."

"But Caressa being in charge would only hurt your bottom line," I argued. I shook my head and watched his index finger, hoping it wouldn't travel any lower than the statue's face. "It certainly couldn't help it."

He shrugged and didn't seem overly concerned. "Be that as it may, I care not," he said while glancing over his shoulder at me again. His attention fell onto the statue once more, and he withdrew his finger from her cheek before holding it in the air. His gaze dropped to her large breasts. "Yes, it will be more challenging to ensure that our ... products are distributed, but where there is a will, I trust we will find a way."

"You still haven't told me why you're taking over the portals," I announced, albeit solemnly because his previous comment didn't exactly thrill me. But then again, most of what came out of Bram's mouth didn't exactly thrill me. And I also couldn't say I was ecstatic with the way he was staring at the statue's breasts, as if he were hoping they would magically morph into warm flesh right in front of him.

He faced me with his straight-lipped expression. "First, you must understand the panic that my and other organizations are suffering from at this most recent change of hands. All of the exporters consider Caressa an imminent threat. None of them can comprehend their futures, or the potential difficulties in exportation, once the ANC has complete control of the government."

"So what does this have to do with you?"

"May I quote someone we both know? 'Stop interrupting me'!" he emphasized with a wide grin. That only irritated me further.

"Ugh," I grumbled as I ate a generous slice of humble pie and waited for him to continue.

"Due to this perceived threat ..." He paused as if he were baiting me and expecting me to interject.

210

Frowning, I made a point of grinding my teeth together, which only made him laugh. "The other organizations have been discussing the notion of joining our forces, and uniting together, thereby actually threatening the power and administration of the ANC. Perhaps Jax already informed you that we must rely on strength in numbers?"

"He did," I answered with a brief nod.

"Bloody blabbermouth," Bram muttered underneath his breath.

"The point, Bram," I reminded him. "Could we please get back to it?"

"Yes," he said with another theatrical sigh. Returning his gaze to the statue, he apparently remembered where his train of thought derailed. "Many of the progressive leaders claimed if ever there was a time to see one of their own in power, now would be it." He took a deep breath as if he needed one and then continued, his eyes still glued to the statue's very alert nipples. "Upon my discovery that these organizations were hedging their bets, and soon planned to see one of their own in power, I realized it had to be nipped in the bud."

"And you expect to accomplish that by taking control of our portals?" I spat out, now nearly unable to restrain myself. "How does that make any freaking sense at all?!" I demanded.

He shook his head, looking at me as if I were a lost cause because I wasn't following him, but the smile on his lips revealed his unbridled amusement. "No, that is not why, Sweet. Please try to control your Tourette Syndrome so I may continue."

"Ha-ha, Bram, that's really funny," I grumbled. "Go on."

"I refused to allow myself to be relegated to the mercy of another leader, or another Melchior O'Neil," he explained, although his eyes never left the statue. Despite my most earnest wishes to the contrary, Bram started tracing the statue's breast with one finger. He drew an imaginary line down to her nipple. Once he reached the erect nub, his finger began circling it.

"As if you could ever be at anyone's mercy," I replied sarcastically before turning away. I definitely didn't want to witness him molesting the statue.

"Yes, you are quite right," he agreed, and his tone of voice sounded like he was literally beaming. "The king of the jungle is the apex predator, and subjugated to nobody!"

"I have no words," I said with a frown as I faced him again, pleased to see he was no longer fondling the statue. Now, his hands hung at his sides and his attention, ostensibly, was mine once again.

"You have no words ... for once!" Bram's quip made him smile wider, like he was proud of himself. Taking a few steps toward me, he put his hands back inside his pockets. "The point, my dear, little Regulator, is that I prefer to avoid any situation that is out of my control. I did the only thing I could do. I took matters into my own hands."

"Which means what, exactly?" I prodded. Trying to keep him on topic at the same time I wanted him to hurry the hell up and spit it out was a tricky trail to follow.

"I had to prove where my loyalty lay," he answered. One of his eyebrows arched up in visible frustration. The whole situation seemed to aggravate Bram to no end, but I still didn't know exactly why. "I had to prove to the exporters that I was willing to work with them, and become the leader they so desperately needed." He was quiet for a few seconds and we just stared at one another. "I had to hoodwink them. I persuaded them to believe I wanted only the best for them."

"But you don't want what is best for them?" I asked, eyeing him narrowly as I tried to fully understand his meaning and once understanding it, decide if he was telling me the truth or not.

"I only want what is best for you, my dear," he replied. Walking right up to me, he jabbed me with his index finger straight in the center of my chest. "At the same time, I also want what is best for *me*."

"Uh-huh ... So your idea was to seize control of the portals just to prove to those organizations that you were assuming the role as their worthy leader?" I finished before taking a step back. I crossed my arms over my chest, just in case he got any other ideas about touching me at breast level.

As far as our conversation was concerned, I was pleased to find that I was starting to piece the puzzle together.

"Yes," he answered immediately. "I had to prove my loyalty to their cause, and it was a way to firmly cement my superiority at the top of the pecking order."

"So where and why do I come into this?"

"I now require your assistance, Sweet," he answered plainly.

I couldn't respond right away because I was so taken aback. I didn't know what to say. I had no idea what kind of assistance I could offer him. Especially when he was well aware how I wanted nothing to do with the illegal potions trade at all. It was just as abhorrent in my eyes as my dead father. As soon as that thought crossed my mind, though, I realized exactly what Bram really wanted.

"You want *me* to help *you* take control of every ANC portal, don't you?" I asked before my jaw dropped in disbelief.

He merely nodded like it wasn't a big deal.

I immediately shot to my feet and shook my head vehemently. When I finally met his eyes, my anger nearly blinded me. "You've completely lost your fucking mind!"

"Stand down, my pet," he crooned with a laugh. Raising his hand, he attempted to get me to calm down, but it didn't work.

"Why do you think I would ever help you to take control of the portals?" I asked, continuing to shake my head all the while because his gall amazed me.

"Because it will be one step in the right direction to repress this rebellion," he answered, straight-lipped.

"You want to repress their rebellion?" I repeated, my tone of voice revealing my doubt. "After earning their trust? After becoming their leader? After facing a position in which you'll be more powerful than you ever have been before? You're going to just throw that all away?"

"Yes," he replied immediately. "I fear it is the only way. This rebellion cannot be allowed to flourish. It must be repressed. But in order to do that, I must first earn their loyalty. Then I will squash them."

I was quiet for a few seconds as I studied him, wondering if he were still being honest with me. Trying to read Bram's true motives was like trying to read hieroglyphics. His poker face was flawless. 'Course, he'd had over three hundred years to perfect it.

"So, my job would be helping you take control of the portals; and then what?" I asked, assuming the role of Devil's Advocate again. Not that I was swayed by his argument, because I wasn't. Not in the least bit. But it was better to understand the full scope of the situation before I made any quick judgements.

"The ANC would be fully aware of our moves," Bram announced, his eyes now riveted to mine. "They would authorize every step before we could take it."

"That doesn't answer my question. After you control the portals, then what?"

"Patience, my Sweet," he answered with a fangy smile that caused a shiver of unease to shutter through me. "Once we seize the portals, we would pretend to begin infiltrating the Netherworld. To those not in the know, it would appear as if we were assuming control of the government by going through the back door."

"And then what?"

"And that would be precisely when the ANC would step in to ensure that would never happen. There would be enough exporters involved in this heist that the ANC could arrest all of them and take them into custody. That would naturally deplete the numbers in the potions organizations and, thus, debilitate and annihilate them," he finished.

"Which would mean the balance between the ANC and the potions rings would be back to how it was before my father ever took office," I summarized after I considered everything Bram said.

"Yes, the balance would be again restored." He eyed me with another winning smile and offered me his hand. I wasn't sure why I allowed him to take mine, but once he did, he pulled me against him and held me tightly.

"What?" I started to protest, but he interrupted me.

"You must ensure that we prevail in our attack for the portals, Sweet. I need you to guarantee our victory."

"And why should I trust you?" I asked. My eyes narrowed as I brought both of my palms against his chest and pushed away from him.

"You should trust me because that is what our relationship has always relied on, or am I mistaken?" He gripped both of my upper arms, ostensibly to keep me in place, and I couldn't help noticing his fangs were now completely elongated and ... sharp.

"I don't know," I said with obvious uncertainty. "You tell me."

He didn't respond as he stared at me, and his eyes appeared bluer than usual. Suddenly, I remembered to immediately close my eyes. I was afraid he would try to bewitch me again. I heard the sound of his deep, resonant chuckling and felt the pad of his thumb touching my left cheek.

"Sweet, please open your lovely emerald eyes," he whispered.

"Why? So you can magick me into doing whatever evil plans you have up your sleeve?" I answered, keeping my eyes sealed tightly.

"You should know me better than that," he said while exhaling deeply, and his cold breath chilled my face.

"I refuse to take any chances where you're concerned, Bram," I admitted. "The day I fully trust the serpent is the day it sinks its fangs into me."

"Were we not just having this conversation, except in reverse? You said, and I quote, *'the only way this rocky relationship will work is by maintaining trust,'*" he finished. I eventually opened my eyes, figuring I could close them again if he tried to overpower me. I didn't have a comment because he'd caught me between a rock and a very hard place. Having someone using your own words against you was beyond irksome.

"I give you my word, as a gentleman, that I will not make any attempt to overpower you," he said in a soft voice.

I hoped my gut instincts weren't off, but his expression seemed earnest. I studied him for another few seconds, poised to slam my eyelids shut if I received even the slightest inkling that he was bluffing. But I didn't.

"You have my word," he repeated, slightly easing his hold on my upper arms. My palms were still flattened against his chest, and I was standing way too close to him, so I cleared my throat and stepped back.

"Everything I have told you is the truth," he stated solemnly. "You were correct; you and I must be honest and straightforward with one another. A truer sentiment was never spoken, especially now. You and I need each other now more than we ever did before."

Neither one of us said anything for a few seconds. We just stared at each other, as if we were trying to assess the truth from each other. For my own part, I wasn't sure how far I could trust Bram. He'd mostly done the right thing in the past, but I still wondered if all of it was just a farce. Maybe he'd been warming me up just to earn my trust. Maybe all of that had just been leading up to this very moment.

The bummer of the whole situation was that there was no way I could know for sure whether Bram was genuine or whether this was all an amazingly well-conceived sham.

"I would never subject you to any precarious situation," he promised, his eyes boring into mine. I had yet to feel his power behind them, though. "Your health and well-being take priority over my own," he claimed.

"Such a heartwarming scene!"

The sound of Jax's voice coincided with him clapping. My heartbeat started to race and I felt light-headed. Looking in the direction of Jax's voice, I saw him standing in the doorway. His enormous physique nearly obscured the entire space. He was glaring at us, his large arms crossed over his substantially broad chest.

Time seemed to stand still as my attention shifted from Jax to Bram. I watched the vampire's entire expression change. His eyes narrowed and his fangs grew longer while his jaw tightened. I could almost feel the sudden rigidity of his body. And then I felt him twitch.

"I wouldn't think about materializing anywhere if I were you, boss," Jax warned him, shaking his head as three more large men suddenly appeared behind him. One of them handed Jax a gun, which I supposed was probably loaded with dragon blood bullets.

At the sound of a door opening, I glanced behind me and saw four men standing at the far end of the room. They were in front of a door I hadn't noticed earlier. The sweat started to bead along my forehead as I strove to catch my breath. Bram took a step in front of me and reached around me, grabbing my arm and pulling me closer to him. He seemed to be shielding me with his own body.

"I'm sure it will please the others when they learn that you consider us nothing more than your *puppets*," Jax hissed as he walked into the room with the three thugs trailing him.

"Whatever grievances you have with me," Bram started, although his tone of voice was surprisingly unconcerned, "leave Dulcie out of it."

Jax chuckled. "Wow, boss, you really must have it bad, don't you?"

Being protected by Bram's body, I couldn't see what was going on. But I heard the sound of heavy footsteps, which were coming closer. Seconds later, Jax stood right in front of me. He held the barrel of what looked like an Op 9 to Bram's temple. Reaching out, he gripped my upper arm, and none-too-gently.

Then he yanked me forward, closer to him, holding me in place by draping his heavy arm across me.

"I mean," Jax continued as he glanced down at me and smirked. "I get it. She's hot. I had a hell of a time persuading myself not to touch her."

"I would sooner die a thousand deaths," I ground out, glaring up at him.

He shrugged. "And it might very well come to that."

"I prefer not to repeat myself," Bram said. His eyes looked icy and his jaw was so tight, I half wondered if he might snap his fangs in half. "Leave her alone!"

"Then save your voice," Jax answered, his jaw just as determined. "Because I need her." Glancing back down at me, he narrowed his eyes. "This little prized possession is going to come in very handy."

Longing for more?
Don't miss Dulcie O'Neil's return in...

GRAVE NEW WORLD
The 8ᵗʰ Book in the Dulcie O'Neil Series
AVAILABLE NOW!

Get FREE E-BOOKS!

It's as easy as:

1. Visit my website www.hpmallory.com

2. Sign up with your email address

3. Download your 4 e-books!

About the Author:

H. P. Mallory is a New York Times and USA Today Bestselling author!

She lives in Southern California with her son and two cranky cats, where she's at work on her next book.

Printed in the USA
CPSIA information can be obtained
at www.ICGtesting.com
LVHW011725261223
767464LV00009B/542